Soul to Soul

Donna Hill

INDIGO

Indigo is an imprint of
Genesis Press, Inc.
315 Third Avenue North
Columbus, Mississippi 39701

Copyright © 2000 by Donna Hill

Soul to Soul

ISBN 1-58571-000-8

Manufactured in the United States of America

FIRST EDITION

Soul to Soul

ONE

It was lunchtime and the black folks of Clinton Hill tumbled out onto the Brooklyn streets, meandering in and out of antique shops, Afrocentric boutiques, and almost upscale restaurants in search of something to do for that one blessed hour.

Leone Weathers had her own agenda as she weaved in and out of the foot traffic on Fulton Street. Her spirits felt as light as the September air that gently tussled her recently cut hair. Her bandleader, and after-hours lover, Cole Fleming, had called to tell her to hurry down to the club and listen to the sax player he'd found.

The club had been without a permanent saxophone player for almost two months, after the last one got a gig touring Europe. She had listened to so many "potential" candidates her ears were crossing. It's not that they weren't good, they just weren't great. They didn't have that "somethin' somethin" that took your breath away. Leone had grown so weary of the search, she'd turned the whole process over to Cole and warned him not to call her until he was positive he'd found "the one." This time he was certain, he'd assured her less than an hour earlier. "Come in and hear him for yourself. You won't be disappointed."

So, she'd thrown on a pair of jeans, a long-sleeve white cotton blouse and her sneakers and hurried over to the club, which was only five blocks away from her house.

Leone stopped in front of the smoked glass door and couldn't help smiling with pride as she looked at the gold leaf lettering on the door: Soul to Soul Nightclub and Restaurant.

Soul to Soul was her baby. She'd worked twenty years as a registered nurse, saved her money and purchased her dream five years earlier—her very own nightclub. She'd put a lot of work into rehabbing the abandoned building and making it into one of the fastest growing hot spots in downtown Brooklyn.

The first year had been a struggle, and between the growing pains of her teenage daughter Raven, the disintegration of her marriage to Steven, and trying to get her business off the ground, there were many days when Leone wanted to throw in the towel and go back to nursing. It was people like Cole, and her best friend and business consultant, Antoinette Lewis, who kept her believing in her dream.

Leone dug into her canvas bag and pulled out her keys. Antoinette had been pressuring her into considering opening for lunch, but Leone had balked at the idea. Dealing with the after-work and dinner crowd was quite enough, she'd said. Maybe in another year, but now was too soon. She'd had enough changes to deal with over the past year or two. With her daughter rapidly approaching eighteen and developing a life of her own, the business pretty much self-sufficient, she'd had a bit more time to look at her own life and where she was. What she was discovering day-by-day had led her to begin rethinking her direction.

She was getting older and in a few more years her forties would be a thing of the past. Cole had been pressuring her to get married, but she'd coyly been able to put him off and wasn't certain why. He was a wonderful man and they had a decent relationship, but at the heart of it, she didn't really think she loved Cole. At least not the kind of love to build a marriage on. She'd been down that road and maybe her disastrous marriage had jaded her to the sanctity of union. But the more she examined her feelings, the more she realized that what she wanted in a relationship was that spark, that total feeling of compatibility that was more than just great sex and someone good to look at in the morning. Yet, the thought of being alone again kept her locked in place.

Unlocking the door, Leone slipped her sunglasses from her nose and stepped into the dim, cool interior.

"Hi Terry," Leone said, waving to her hostess. Leone continued toward the back of the nightclub. "Where's Cole?" she asked over her shoulder.

"I think he's in the office," Terry said over the din of glasses and dishes clattering in the kitchen.

"Thanks."

Leone walked around the circular tables until she'd made her way to the office. The door was partially opened and she could hear male voices coming from inside. One she knew with her eyes closed, the other she didn't recognize, its deep pulsing quality suddenly making her feel warm all over. Leone pushed the door open and stepped inside.

Cole was seated behind the desk. He looked up when Leone walked in. A slow smile and a hint of something a bit more intimate spread across his dark brown face. The one with the voice had his back turned toward her. The shoulders were wide, stretched beneath a blue denim shirt, she quickly observed. His hair was neatly trimmed, cut close to his head and she knew the almost carnal scent she smelled was not Cole. Her stomach did an inexplicable tumble before settling down.

Leone closed the door and stepped fully into the room. "Hey, Cole."

Cole stood and the stranger turned in his seat. The dark probing eyes with the slightly hooded brow and slick black lashes, made an all too appealing picture set against his warm brandy-toned skin. His full mouth, lined by a thin mustache, dipped in the center like a heart to tease the lush bottom lip that he languidly licked with a swipe of his tongue.

"Leone, this is the man I was talking to you about. Ray Taylor. Ray, Leone Weathers."

The stranger stood, extending his hand simultaneously. "You're definitely the lady of the house. Cole, here," he added with a toss of his head, "has been singing your praises all morning."

Leone felt her hand become enveloped by his. "Cole tends to exaggerate," she said derisively, trying to ignore the warm pressure of his hand. "But in your case I hope he proves me wrong. He says you're the player we've been looking for."

"I believe I am," Ray said without pretext. "It's what I do." His gaze of challenge burned into her eyes.

She raised her chin a notch. "And how long have you been doing it?"

The corner of his mouth curved in a wicked grin and his eyes suddenly picked up the light. "Since I was big enough to hold the instrument in my hands and make it do what I wanted—or what was asked." The challenge in his voice, the languid assurance of his body, the unfathomable thing in his eyes, held her on the precipice of temptation, almost daring her to take the leap. Right then. Don't look back.

Leone felt her face heat, and the flush spread through her body. The conversation was benign, she reasoned, over the frightening racing of her heart. It was the tone and the double entendre of the banter that raised the stakes to something infinitely more dangerous.

Cole chuckled and came from behind the desk, effectively short-circuiting the electric current that zinged back and forth between Leone and Ray. "If you like what you hear, I figured Ray could sit in on a set tonight," Cole said, watching Leone closely.

She turned to him, freeing herself of the erotic web of words. "I don't think he needs an audition." Did they hear the breathlessness in her voice? she wondered. "If you say he's good, I'll take your word for it. The audience will be the final judge." She threw down the gauntlet. "Give him a solo tonight. Let's see what he can do."

Leone gave Ray a cursory glance. "Nice meeting you. If it works out you'll be dealing with Cole. What he says goes."

"I'm sure it will," Ray offered.

Leone turned to leave. The room had grown infinitely smaller. "Cole, can I see you outside?"

Cole stepped out of the office and shut the door behind him. His cool brown complexion had hints of red undertones, an early indication that he was upset about something.

"What the hell was that about in there?" he asked from between his teeth, hooking his finger over his shoulder toward the office.

Leone's eyes sharpened. "What are you talking about?"

"You know perfectly well what I'm talking about. You two were no more talking about playing the sax than you were about the theory of evolution."

"What!" She planted her hands on her hips. "Now you've really lost it."

"Lost it. Didn't you see him coming on to you—and you letting him? How's that supposed to make me feel, Leone, huh? What am I, the invisible man or something?"

Leone let out a sigh, knowing full well that Cole had hit the mark. The very idea that she'd been so transparent made her feel every bit like the kind of woman other women whisper about in not so pleasant terms. She'd just about made a fool of herself in there and made a fool of him as well. She and Cole had been an item for more than a year. They were more than business partners, they were lovers. It was a comfortable relationship. She didn't see rockets go off every time they made love, or feel her stomach do flips when she heard his voice on the phone, but Cole was good to her and to Raven. He was solid, the kind of man women spend their lives looking for. Sure, he had his faults, shortcomings and baggage; but didn't everyone? She had no reason to look elsewhere, and she wasn't quite sure why, for that moment in the office, she did.

She stepped up to Cole, reached out and stroked his cheek, the beginning of afternoon stubble tickling her palm. She ran her hand across his short salt and pepper hair, looked into his soft brown eyes. Yes, she was content. Wasn't she?

"Cole, babe, you're letting your imagination play tricks on you. There's no more happening between me and that man than me and that broomstick in the corner. This is business. Simple." Her voice grew softer. "Don't take this someplace it doesn't need to go."

Cole stared at her a moment, trying to see beyond the words. He laughed softly. "Maybe it is me. I'm kinda old to be playing the jealous lover, huh?"

"Tell you the truth, I'm flattered. I can't remember the last time a man got jealous about me."

Cole stepped closer, cutting off all available space between them. "Any man in their right mind should know what a catch you are, Lee. They'd be a fool if they didn't." He let his hand trail down her arm. "It would make a man crazy to think that someone else had their eye on you."

"Well, that's not something you have to worry about," she said, pressing her finger to his chest. She checked her watch. "I need to run home. I want to see Raven before she goes out tonight. It's a double date thing and I want to be sure everything is correct."

"She still crazy about that guy Ron?"

They began to walk toward the exit.

"She is for this week," Leone laughed. "Who knows? I must admit, he has hung around longer than some of the others." She looked thoughtful for a moment, then gazed up at Cole. "I don't know if that's a good thing or not. I mean, she's only seventeen. She's still too young to become serious with anyone. That only spells trouble."

Cole draped his arm around her shoulder. "Raven is a good kid, Leone. You raised her right. She'll keep her head on straight."

"I hope so. I just pray that she doesn't become a statistic like so many young girls."

"Raven gets plenty of love and support. She does-
n't have to go out looking for it. Just relax and let her
be a teenager."

Leone sighed. "I guess you're right." She raised up
and pecked his lips. "You usually are."

Cole opened the door for her. "I know," he teased.

"I'll see you later. About ten." She walked outside,
slid on her shades and headed home. But even as she
did, thoughts of Ray Taylor dogged her trail.

TWO

Ray Taylor sat with his right ankle resting on his left knee, staring at the posters and flyers tacked to the office wall. There was also row of framed portraits capturing a variety of media stars and musicians who'd visited the club at one time or another. In each of them there was a picture of Leone Weathers, in outfits from casual to sequin-studded.

The montage of pictures gave Ray some insight into a very intriguing woman. She appeared to be just as comfortable in paint-spattered jeans as she did in formal dinner wear, and everything in-between.

He ran his index finger along the line of his mustache, wondering just exactly what the relationship was between Cole and Leone. He sensed something. Cole took on a proprietary air when Leone entered the room. Interesting, he'd thought, when he watched Cole stake out his territory. But was it really his, or only wishful thinking?

"Sorry I took so long," Cole said, entering the room and derailing Ray's thoughts. He turned in his chair.

"No problem, man. I was just checking out the pictures. A lot of big names have come through here."

Cole chuckled. "That's all Leone's doing. She's a master at getting beyond the secretaries and right to the source. Once she gets it in her head she wants to invite someone to Soul to Soul, believe me, it's a done deal. After the first year or so, folks started calling her, wanting to know when it was a good night to drop by, or they'd stop in when they were in town."

"She seems like a very determined lady."

Cole assessed Ray a moment, trying to hear something beneath the words, see some giveaway in his eyes. Ray's expression remained relaxed and open. "Yes. That she is." He came around the desk. "We start rehearsal at three. Happy hour starts at five, but we just play CDs until the band comes on at nine."

Ray nodded. "No problem." He stood. "I'll be here. I'm just going to grab some lunch."

Cole reached into his desk and pulled out a sheaf of papers. "Do you read music?"

"Enough."

Cole handed the stack to Ray. "Here's what we'll be playing tonight. Take a look, and if you have any questions, we'll go over them at rehearsal."

Ray tucked the folder under his arm. "See you in a few."

Cole watched Ray walk out and wondered if he'd just hired pure brilliance or just plain trouble.

Leone stopped in the cleaners to pick up the dress for Raven and realized she was starving. She still had at least an hour before Raven got in and began to panic about her dress. So she decided to visit her favorite African restaurant and grab one of their famous steamed vegetable pita sandwiches and some fruit juice.

The décor was simple and airy with small round tables strategically placed around the room. African artwork and straw mats hung from the walls. The entire side of the building was glass, giving the diners a great view of the passersby and the art gallery across the street.

Having been served with her meal, Leone pulled a copy of the Amsterdam News out of her bag and sat back to enjoy her food. The things she liked most about the small eatery were that it was pristine clean, never too crowded and the food was excellent. And she secretly wanted to find out the recipe for the steamed veggies.

Leone glanced up from her reading just as Ray Taylor strolled by the window. Her insides suddenly knotted, the same way they'd felt whenever she would see Chris Lawrence, the senior basketball star, walk through the halls of her high school, and pray that he would notice her and say hello.

And then Ray was gone, moving casually down the street, blending in with the other pedestrians. Leone released a breath she hadn't realized she'd held. An overwhelming urge to leave and try to catch up with him, ask him where he was going, where he'd been, what his plans were for the future, mysteriously pushed her up out of her seat.

She shook her head, snapping good sense back into place. What is wrong with you? she silently chastised herself. You don't know that man from a banana plant. She slowly sat back down and tried to concentrate on her food, but had lost her appetite. Distracted, she pushed the plate away, dug in her purse for some money and paid the check.

When she came outside, she secretly hoped that perhaps he might be standing outside peering into a shop window. Casually, she looked up and down the block. Ray Taylor was nowhere to be seen. It was probably for the best anyway.

∞

"You look beautiful, sweetheart," Leone told her daughter.

Raven twirled around in her teal mini-dress and grinned broadly, displaying the deep dimples she'd inherited from her father. She planted her hands on her hips. "But I don't want to be beautiful, I want to be fly," she announced with flair.

"Excuse me. Fly, then," Leone conceded drolly. "What time are they picking you up?"

"Six-thirty. Terry said they were on their way."

"What's the name of this place you're going to again?"

"Gee Ma, you must be getting old. I told you like three times already. Harvest House. Terry's mom rented a room for the night for Terry's brother's twenty-first birthday party. Dinner at eight, party after. Remember?"

"Right." Leone tucked her hair behind her ears and stared unseeing at the magazine on her lap.

"Is something wrong? You've been acting weird since you came home."

Leone looked up and pasted a bland look on her face. "No. I'm fine."

Raven stared at her mother for a minute longer. "Daddy didn't call and upset you again, did he?"

"No, your father didn't call. And what makes you think his calls upset me?"

"Because they do. You know it and I know it."

"Maybe you know too much. Ever think of that?"

"I only wish."

The doorbell rang.

"That must be them," Raven said, grabbing her bag from the glass table and dashing toward the door, her shoulder-length hair swinging behind her.

Leone pulled herself up from the comfort of her couch and walked toward the door.

"Hi, Ms. Weathers," Terry greeted, giving Leone a quick kiss on the cheek.

"Hi, honey. How's your mom?"

"Fine. She's downstairs in the van."

Ron stepped out from behind Terry. "Hi, Ms. Weathers," he said in his getting-manly voice.

Leone gave him a quick once-over. As usual, he was impeccably dressed in his oversized designer clothes that made his long, lanky body even longer and lankier.

"Hello, Ronald. Good to see you."

"Hi, Ron," Raven cooed, and took his hand, which caused him to blush beneath his cool olive tones.

"Hey, you look fly," he mumbled, and Raven turned a triumphant smile on her mother.

"We better get going," Raven said.

"Your mother is going to bring you all back, right?" Leone asked, directing her question to Terry.

"Yes, Ms. Weathers."

"All right, then. Have a good time. And don't forget to act like a lady, Raven."

Raven kissed her mother's cheek. "You sure know how to take the fun out of an evening," she joked. "See you later and don't work too hard tonight."

"Night, Ms. Weathers," Terry and Ron said in unison and the trio bounded off down the stairs.

Leone returned to the living room, picked up the magazine from the black couch and returned it to the wicker magazine rack near the loveseat. She fluffed the mud-cloth pillows and returned them to couch. Walking around the table, she headed into her bedroom to get ready for her evening.

While she showered and then spent some time applying lotion to her damp body, her thoughts continued to drift back to Ray Taylor. She hadn't thought to ask Cole too many questions about him. Since she'd implemented her hands-off policy, she'd left all the details up to Cole. Now she wished she hadn't.

Leone stood and stared at her nude body in the mirror. What was it about Ray Taylor that had captured her imagination? A better and more troubling question was, why didn't she feel the same charge when she looked into Cole's eyes?

"This is ridiculous." She slipped on her underwear. "I have a man," she fussed. "A good man at that. Other women would kill to have someone like Cole." She sat on the bed and put on her stockings. "He loves me and he loves Raven. Ray Taylor is just an interesting stranger." Who am I trying to convince?

She took her gray knit dress from the hanger and slid it over her head. The clingy fabric caressed the curves of her long body. Leone smiled at her reflection. "Not bad for a woman pushing fifty."

Twenty minutes later she was walking out the door.

By the time Leone arrived at Soul to Soul the club was quite full. The bar was lined from one end to the other and there were fewer than a dozen tables available.

She greeted some of the familiar faces as she made her way around the club. Her first stop, as always, was the kitchen, to ensure that everything was running smoothly and that the cooks weren't on the brink of slicing each other to bits arguing over a recipe.

Confident that everything was under control, she made a quick pit stop to chat with her head hostess, Kelly. Kelly had been with the club since the beginning, although her real love was modeling. She'd actually landed some print-ads and more jobs had begun to crop up everyday. Leone knew it was only a matter of time before Kelly made it big and moved on. She dreaded the moment. Kelly wasn't only great to look at, she had a dynamite personality and knew how to run the club with her eyes closed.

"How's everything going?" Leone asked, catching up with Kelly at the check-in table.

Kelly looked up from the list of reservations and smiled brightly, her green eyes sparkling in the light.

"Hi, Lee. Busy as usual, girl. I had to put Percy in check about the menu. It seems he had his own ideas about what jerk shrimp was supposed to be. I got that straight quick."

Leone chuckled, imagining the throw down between her head hostess and her head chef. Egos to go. "I know you did. Anything else I need to know?"

"Yeah, you need to get a bigger place. In another year, we'll be busting at the seams. Every week it seems that ten more people hear about Soul to Soul and bring ten of their friends."

"Word of mouth is the best advertiser."

"Well, folks need to stop talkin' just for a minute, so I can catch my breath."

The two women laughed.

"Ooh, have you met the new sax player?" Kelly asked under her breath.

Leone's chest tightened for a moment. "Yeah, I...uh...met him this afternoon. Is there a problem?"

"Other than the brother being too fine for his own good and the fact that every unescorted, red-blooded woman coming through here has tried to get his attention? No, there's no problem."

"I'm sure the interest will dwindle once he's been here for a while and folks get used to seeing him," Leone offered, hoping more than stating fact.

"Humph. I doubt it."

A young couple approached the table and Leone made her quick goodbye and moved on.

So, Ray Taylor was making an impression already, Leone mused, her heels clicking rhythmically as she headed for the back office. She wondered if he played half as good as he looked. She twisted her wrist and checked the time. Well, another half hour and she'd know for herself.

THREE

"Hey, babe," Cole greeted, looking up from the payroll sheets when Leone entered the office.

"How's everything?" She came into the room and put her purse on the desk, then gave Cole a light peck on the cheek.

"Another busy night," he said. "Did Raven get off okay?"

Leone propped her hip on the edge of the desk. "Terry and Ron came to pick her up. What are you doing?" she asked, peeking over his bent head.

"Adding Ray Taylor's name to the payroll sheet. I'll put all the particulars in the computer tomorrow. I didn't get a chance today."

"I could do it. I'll be in early tomorrow," she offered, hoping she didn't sound too anxious.

He glanced up at her. "Sure, if you want to." He leaned back in the seat. "I think he'll work out great. We had a fantastic rehearsal and he fit right it." He slowly shook his head in amazement. "Taylor has a style that is totally unique. He's a combination of Dexter Gordon and Coltrane. Lethal. Hope we can hold on to him. I can see big things in his future."

"Really," Leone stated, reaching for a blasé tone. "If you believe it, then it must be so."

"Thanks for the vote of confidence, Madame Boss Lady. And on that note, I need to get ready for the first set." He stood, looking at her with desire brimming in his eyes. "You look fabulous, babe." He leaned down and kissed her exposed neck. "Can't wait for the night to be over," he whispered against her flesh. "Is Raven coming home or spending the night at Terry's?"

"She's coming home."

"Hmmm. So much for that idea. Maybe you can make some time for me later. I promise I won't keep you up too late."

She managed a shaky smile. "Let's see how the night goes." She stroked his cheek. "And take it from there."

Cole angled his head to the side. "Are you all right? You seem distracted."

She quickly stood, averting her gaze. "I'm fine."

He waited a beat. "Okay. But think about what I said." He ran his hand down her arm. "It's been awhile, and I'm missing you. Know what I mean?"

"I know. Me, too. We'll see, okay?"

"All right. Let me get going. Check with you later."

Leone watched him walk out and a kind of sadness settled over her when she quietly admitted to herself that she wasn't looking forward to spending the latter part of her night in Cole's arms.

The house lights dimmed and the spot shone on the six piece band. The packed house settled down, reducing conversation to a low hum as Cole stepped up to the microphone.

"Welcome, sisters and brothers. As always, I can guarantee you're in for a night of soulful entertainment. I want you to put your hands together for our newest band member who I know will delight you. Let's hear it for Ray Taylor on sax."

To the sound of applause and foot stomping, Ray moved like a lapping wave, smooth and easy, toward the front of the stage, his long, lean body outfitted in all-black. His smile was enough to dazzle the crowd, but he took them to another level as he led off with a solo of "In a Sentimental Mood," by John Coltrane.

Heads rocked and feet tapped as he took them through the strains of the moody classic before being joined by the rest of the band. They played non-stop for more than an hour, tossing in some Miles Davis, Illinois Jacquet, Lionel Hampton, Wynton Marsalis, Earl "Fatha" Hynes, Dizzy Gillespie, and Lester Young. The crowd roared their approval and Cole promised more of the same during the second set.

Leone enjoyed the music with everyone else, but her attention was riveted on Ray. When he stepped to the microphone and began to play, something akin to magic filled the air. He mesmerized the audience—not only with the sound of his sax, but with his very presence. There was an undeniable charisma about Ray that couldn't be ignored. Ray Taylor had star quality and the women in the room smelled it from miles away.

Leone stayed in the corner of the room, where she'd taken up her post when the band came on, and watched the hungry females go on the prowl. The instant he set foot offstage and walked onto the floor, three women from various points in the club made their way to him.

They looked to be not much older than their late twenties, with the tight bodies of youth and no childbirth. Leone glanced at her profile in the walled mirror. There was no doubt that she'd passed twenty a couple of times and that her once dancer-trim body had bid her a fond farewell. She sucked in her stomach. It helped a little, but she obviously couldn't hold her breath for the entire night.

"The new guy is on the money," Kelly shouted over the din, easing alongside Leone.

Leone snapped her head in Kelly's direction. "Not bad."

"Not bad? Girl, he has it going on. And look at the women trying to get next to him," she added, angling her head toward the bar.

Ray was leaning casually against the bar, with a glass in one hand, his other tucked in his pocket while he held court. One woman, who easily resembled Tara Banks, was close enough to see the pores in his skin, Leone observed with a twinge. Two others braced him on the opposite side. What was even more amazing was that Ray seemed totally unfazed by the attention. He appeared to truly enjoy it, as if it were commonplace, even expected somehow. The very notion rubbed Leone the wrong way.

She pursed her lips. With all that talent, all his looks and personality, why was he working in a small club like Soul to Soul? she suddenly wondered. It would seem that someone like Ray Taylor would be with a big band or recording on his own somewhere. Curious, she thought.

"Well, let me tend to the masses," Kelly said. "See you later." She moved away, then stopped and shouted over her shoulder, "Cole was looking for you. I think he's up front."

Leone waved her thanks. She took a breath and peered over heads in search of Cole and spotted him at a booth talking with two of the band members. Leone wound her way around the plaster pillars and tables until she reached where Cole was sitting.

Cole smiled broadly when she approached and slid over on the red leather seat to make room for her.

"So what did you think, babe? He as good as I said he was?"

"You were right. He definitely has talent," she said aloud. In more ways than one, she wanted to add but didn't. "All of you were fantastic tonight. Turned the place out." She smiled at Keith, the piano player, and Mark, the drummer.

"This is the man," Keith said, raising his glass to Cole. "He's the one who puts the sounds together. We're just his humble servants."

The group chuckled.

Leone slid her arm around his shoulder. "Don't work your humble servants too hard. You all were throwing off so much energy, you practically had folks levitating."

"I hope that's a good thing," Ray said, suddenly standing above them.

Leone's stomach did a quick dive then settled. Unconsciously, she eased closer to Cole. "Congratulations," she offered. "The crowd loves you."

Ray's mouth cocked into a half smile. "I feed off their energy," he said, staring intently at Leone. His eyes picked up the light and shimmered. "And then I try to give it back to them."

She took a quick sip of Cole's rum and coke to ease the sudden dryness in her throat. "Whatever works, and apparently it does." She briefly glanced around the table. "Gentleman, you'll have to excuse me, but some of us have work to do and can't lounge around for hours at a stretch."

A moan rounded the table.

She had to squeeze by Ray in order to get past him, and she caught the scent of his cologne mixed with exertion and raw animal energy. Her heart knocked. "Have a great set," she said and walked away.

For the rest of the evening, Leone caught glimpses of Ray as he mingled with the guests as if he were the resident celebrity. And the more she saw of him, the more she decided he was nothing more than a pretty boy with some talent. It was obvious that he was out to make as many conquests as possible without breaking any speed laws. She'd lost count of the number of women who'd slipped him their number. He's a player, as Raven would say, which was fine with her as long as it didn't interfere with his performance, her business, or her, she thought, slapping down a packet of receipts and tallying up the first set of numbers for the night. Business was booming.

"Hey, why don't you leave that until tomorrow, babe," Cole said, stepping into the office and closing the door behind him. "I know you have to be beat. It was crazy in here tonight."

Leone forced a smile. "I'd rather get it out of the way."

Cole came around to her side of the desk. "It's not a request, Lee." He covered her hand with his to still her fingers on the calculator.

"You know how I hate leaving things half done..."

"This one time won't matter. It's nearly two o'clock. Put everything in the safe and let me take you home. It'll keep."

She sucked on her bottom lip with her teeth.

"Come on. Let me take care of you for a change." He began to massage her neck, something he knew she loved, and he was rewarded with the sound of her heavy sigh.

Leone let her eyes slide shut and allowed Cole to work his magic.

"You know you need to let me take the stress out of your whole body, not just this beautiful neck," Cole uttered, sliding his fingers along her collarbone.

Leone's eyes flew open and she halted the steady trail of his hands toward her breasts. "Not tonight, Cole. Really."

His hands stopped their exploration but didn't release her. "I see." Slowly he stepped back and came around to look at her. "What is it, Lee, really? For weeks now you've been getting more and more distant. When I come near you lately, you act like I shouldn't. What have I done?"

Her throat tightened. She didn't want to hurt Cole. Heaven knows she didn't. She wished she did have some pat answer, some quick solution to what was happening between them, to her, but she didn't.

Briefly she lowered her head. "I don't know what it is, Cole," she said barely above a whisper.

"Do you still have feelings for me, Lee?"

She looked into his eyes. "Of course I do. You know that. I, I'm just tired. Nothing's changed between us, really."

Cole nodded. "Then that's all I have to go on." He tilted up her chin with the tip of his finger. "I'm a patient man, Lee. And you know I love you. I'm willing to wait it out. Just not too long." He paused a beat. "Good night. I'll call you in the morning, see how Raven's date was." He turned to leave, closing the door softly behind him.

Guilt stabbed her with his last comment. She sat there for several minutes thinking about what Cole said, trying to search out what was in her heart, but the image wouldn't come clear.

∞

Over the next few weeks, Leone would have sworn in court that Ray Taylor had a built-in magnet that drew the women to the club. Some nights it was standing room only and Ray continued to charm everyone who crossed his path. She should have been elated that the club was doing such phenomenal business. Cole couldn't seem to stop raving about Ray Taylor, which only added to her angst.

Fortunately, between rehearsals and Leone's often hectic schedule she rarely saw Ray alone, until one afternoon when he came to the club early while Leone was going over the inventory.

"Hello, Ms. Lady," he greeted, coming up behind her as she stood at the bar.

Her pulse quickened as she slowly turned toward the sound of his voice. "It's Leone and you're early, Mr. Taylor." She turned back to what she was doing, and was certain the room had grown warmer.

He eased alongside her and leaned against the bar. "I wanted to get some practice time in before the rest of the guys got here. It's not a problem, is it...Leone?" He half-smiled at her.

Leone kept her eyes focused on her paperwork. "I don't see how it should be."

He dipped his head to get beneath her gaze. Startled, her head jerked upward. A frown planted itself on her face.

"That's better. It's really hard talking to someone who seems to be ignoring you."

Leone blew out a breath and rested a hand on her hip. "I'm really busy, Mr. Taylor."

"Ray."

"Hmm. You said you came to practice. So..."

"Have I done something to you? I mean everyone else is friendly, chatty, except you. Since my first day you've barely said two words to me. What is it?"

"Are you saying I'm rude, that I've somehow treated you unfairly?"

"No. That's not what I'm saying at all. It's just that—"

"Then we don't have a problem. Perhaps I may seem distracted, or inattentive, but I have a business to run, which I take very seriously. I'm sure you're accustomed to people running behind you, but I'm not that kind of woman...person."

He looked at her for a moment. "Actually, I'm glad you're not. Don't work too hard." He turned and headed for the stage.

Leone took slow breaths, in and out. She put pen to paper and noticed that her hand trembled ever so slightly. Reluctantly, she turned in Ray's direction and watched him as he sauntered toward the stage. She'd done everything in her power to stay as far out of Ray Taylor's reach as possible. She couldn't deny the attraction she felt for him, right from the beginning. But she was too old to be "one of many" for any man. Besides, she had a man. A good one. Why do I have to keep reminding myself of that? she wondered.

Ray stepped on stage, as comfortable there as in his own skin, and took a seat on the lone stool. The music came then, like a lullaby, soft, sweet. The notes of "The Masquerade Is Over" floated through the room as gentle as a breeze, as clear and sharp as if the notes were actually being sung by Sarah Vaughan.

Ray closed his eyes, becoming one with the music, and one by one everybody stopped what they were doing, transfixed by the serene beauty of his playing.

Leone felt her chest fill with an incredible warmth, as captivated as everyone else by the power of his delivery. Could anyone who had such a sense of perfection, who could transform symbols on a piece of paper into something magical, be as shallow as he projected himself to be? Even as she considered the question, Ray took them on another musical odyssey with "Smoke Gets in Your Eyes."

It was just the music, she told herself, picking up her papers and heading toward her office. It wasn't Ray Taylor, the man, who was appealing, who awakened her senses. He was just talented that's all, and she wouldn't fool herself into believing anything else. No matter what her emotions were saying.

FOUR

"So how long has it been this way with you and Cole?" Antoinette asked as she and Leone shared lunch several days later. She chewed on a stalk of celery with blue cheese dressing.

Leone shrugged helplessly, toying with her salad. "Long enough for it to be a problem." She took a sip of her iced tea and let her gaze wander off. "It's not that I don't care, I do. It's just that…" She fumbled for an explanation.

"There's no spark," Antoinette filled in and signaled the waitress for another diet Coke.

"Exactly. Cole is wonderful, don't get me wrong, but…" She hesitated and turned searching eyes on her friend. "Is it wrong for me, at my age, to want to be thrilled by the sight of my man, totally turned on by the thought of his touch? Am I wrong to want that?"

"Of course not." Antoinette's honey brown eyes focused on Leone. "We all deserve to be totally happy in our relationships, Lee, to feel fulfilled, especially at our age. We don't have as much time for the hit and miss of youth. You don't want to simply settle because it's easy and comfortable."

Leone and Antoinette had been friends since high school. For some inexplicable reason they'd gravitated toward each other, as opposites often do. Where Leone was reserved and conventional, Antoinette lived life without restrictions. They were just as opposite in their appearance. Leone was tall, dark brown and moderately built. Antoinette, on the other hand, was a mere five-foot, four with a brick-house body that she had no problem showing off. Yet in every way they complemented each other.

"So what do you think I should do about Cole?" Leone finally asked.

"I think you need to decide if you want to be happy or just satisfied. And when you decide—is Cole the man that can do the trick?"

She watched Leone over the top of her glass. "There's something else going on with you. You know I can always tell from that line." She pointed toward Leone's head. "The one that runs right between your brows. Dead giveaway. Just because I've been away for a month doesn't mean I've forgotten the signs."

Leone tried to shrug it off but knew it was point-less. Antoinette would harass her until she spilled the beans. She had missed talking with Antoinette, espe-cially during the last few weeks. There had been no one with whom she could share her confusion. Yet, sitting in front of her now, it was hard to get the words out. She inhaled deeply and plunged in.

"You know Cole was looking for a new sax player?" she asked, a slight hitch of hesitation in her voice.

"Yes..." Antoinette dragged out, eyeing her suspi-ciously.

Leone cleared her throat. "Well, I met him and..."

"And what?"

"Something happened to me inside," she blurted out. "Something I haven't felt in ages—never felt for Cole, at least not like this."

Antoinette leaned back in her seat, momentarily speechless. Several moments ticked by.

"Don't just sit there. Say something," Leone snapped.

"I'm trying. I'm trying. Every clear thought in my head just took a hike. You, Ms. Cool and in control, having your heart go pitter patter is enough to shut anyone up. Even me."

Leone folded her arm. "I knew I shouldn't have said anything."

"Hey, I'm sorry. You surprised me, that's all. You've always kept your feelings on a short leash. Even on your wedding day, your bridal party seemed more excited than you."

"That doesn't mean I don't feel anything," she said truculently. "I've just never been that way, especially over a man."

Antoinette ignored the bite in her tone and posed her question in soothing strokes, knowing that it was pure anxiety that had Lee on edge. "So what makes this one any different?"

Leone forced herself to relax and regroup, silently embarrassed by her short burst of irrational temper. "I don't really know, Nettie," she said, using the pet name in lieu of an outright apology—an olive branch. "Something just hit me and I haven't been able to get him out of my mind."

"What's his name?"

"Ray Taylor." She hesitated about telling her the last bit of information. As she'd promised Cole, she'd updated the employee files with Ray's background information and to her great dismay discovered that he was ten years younger than she. She'd been walking around for weeks with that little tidbit, and perhaps it contributed to her anxiety over her feelings, knowing that he was younger. As a result, she'd been

standoffish and distant while she battled with the
right and wrong of it. But she figured she might as
well spill the beans at this point. After all, Antoinette
was her best friend. "He's only thirty-eight," she said
almost to herself.

Antoinette's eyes formed two perfect circles. "Say
what?"

"Don't make me say it again." She shoved a plum
tomato into her mouth.

Antoinette threw her head back and howled with
laughter. The couple at the next table looked at her
with disdain for disturbing them.

"I'm leaving," Leone said in a huff, wiping her
mouth with the napkin and tossing it on the table.

"No...no, wait... I'm sorry," Antoinette mumbled
over her laughter, struggling to get it under control.
She wiped her eyes, which had begun to tear up.
"Whew, girl...when you have a story to tell it's a whop-
per." She held up her slender, always manicured
hands. "Okay, okay, I'm cool now." She took a breath.
"So you got a thing for this young brother?"

"You don't have to put it like that."

"Hey, the way I look at it, if you can do it, why not?
Men do it all the time. Look at you. You look just as
good if not better than some of those women that run
in and out of the club. And you're mature. You have
something to offer."

"Whoa, slow down. I didn't say I was going to pursue anything with him."

"Why not?"

"For one thing, I'm with someone."

"Someone that doesn't particularly rock your world
if I remember correctly."

"But he's good to me and to Raven. I don't want to hurt Cole. And I don't really know anything about Ray Taylor. Other than I think he's a player," she mumbled, but not low enough to keep it from Antoinette's eagle ears.

"A player! You've got to be kidding. What makes you say that?"

Leone ran down the events of the club from the time she and Ray formally met to the all-out pursuit of him throughout every night and his apparent enjoyment of it.

"Hmmm. Brother must have it going on," she said with a crooked smile. "I need to meet him."

Leone rolled her eyes. "Which is all the more reason for me to keep my distance."

"But you said he came on to you. Didn't he?"

"Yes, sort of but..."

"Hey, let me tell you something. You only live once. And during that one lifetime you're entitled to some happiness. If you like the guy, go for it." She dipped another celery stalk and pointed it at Leone for emphasis. "Don't let age be a factor. You never know. He could be the one."

Leone pondered her friend's not necessarily wise words. "But what about Cole?"

"Maybe it's time you and Cole had a real talk about how you feel and where the relationship is going...or isn't."

Leone knew Antoinette was right and she dreaded the thought.

∽∾

Ray was lounging on the couch watching Sunday afternoon football with his buddy Parker, but his mind wasn't on the game. He adjusted his body and the soft leather moved with him. The twenty-seven inch television was one big blur of color.

"Touchdown!" Parker shouted, leaping from the chair and doing his own version of a victory dance. "Did you see that? My man rushed for one hundred yards!"

His exclamation was met with silence. Parker craned his neck to stare at Ray.

"Whatsup, man? Did you see that?"

"I wasn't really paying attention," Ray answered absently.

Parker stepped over and placed his hand on Ray's forehead. "No fever," he said sarcastically. "But something's wrong. You've been in a daze since I got here." He sat down. "What? The ladies got you down? Hit a wrong note on the sax? What?"

He shook his head in dismissal. "It's nothing."

Parker stared at him a minute. He and Ray had been running partners since college. Ray pursued his musical career, and Parker went on to business management and financial planning, serving as a consultant for several Fortune 500 corporations, foregoing a solid music career as a pianist. He was instrumental in keeping Ray's finances straight and steering him toward the right stocks and investments. As a result, Ray's future was secure. He would never have to worry about money if he lived two lifetimes. Yet, Ray lived his life as if each day was his last—wanting to get the most, the best, the fastest—from cars and clothes to women. For a man who had so much going for him, he never seemed truly settled inside. He was still the insecure guy from the projects who was never sure what tomorrow was going to bring.

"Hey, if you say it's nothing then I have to go by that. Even though I don't believe it." He leaned toward the coffee table and picked up his beer.

Ray cupped his hands behind his head and stared up at the stucco ceiling. "I'm tired, Parker."

Parker cocked his head. "Tired of what, playing?"

"Everything. Just tired of running from one club to the next, one woman to the next."

"Humph. I thought you loved that life, man. That's what you've been telling me for the past ten years. You love the idea of not being tied down. Hitting and running as you put it."

"Yeah, I did. At least I thought I did."

"So what's different now?"

"I've been doing some thinking for a while. I want to slow down and really see life, ya know. Not have it run past me."

"You're too young for a mid-life crisis. So that's not it. You have some problem with a woman? Somebody snag you and you didn't tell me?"

Ray chuckled half-heartedly. "Naw. The other night at the club—man, it was just like all the others. I got the rush from being on stage. I felt charged, ya know. But then when I was finished the women were everywhere. I played along. At first it was fun, flattering. But it got tiring real quick." He turned and looked at Parker. "The scary part was, I didn't know any other way to be but 'on'. And I just didn't feel like playing the game."

"I think I need another beer." Parker got up and went into the kitchen, returning shortly with two icy cold beers. He handed one to Ray.

"Now that you've reached this pivotal crossroads, what are you going to do? Let's be for real, Ray. You're a musician, a damned good one. You have enough charm to bottle and sell. Women have been on your tail for as long as I've known you, and watching you play is enticing to them. It's all part of the program, the life. It's what brings them back to pack the house."

"Yeah, I know. But I'd like to be able to come home to someone at night, Parker, not bring someone home for the night."

"You're serious, aren't you?"

Ray nodded.

"Wow." He paused, momentarily speechless by this revelation. Finally he collected his thoughts. "So, what are you going to do?"

Ray chuckled. "That's the hard part. I don't know how to play it straight. It's like a foreign language."

"Yeah, the hardest part of anything is getting started. Set your sights on someone—sincerely—and see where it goes. There has to be someone out of the dozens of women you date that you really care about."

Ray did a mental checklist. "Not really. At least not like that." He thought about Leone Weathers, that smile, the challenge in her eyes. That was a woman, and nothing like what he'd been used to.

"Okay, spill it. Who is she? I can tell by the look in your eyes, brother." Parker turned off the television with the remote. The game could wait.

The corner of Ray's mouth quirked briefly upward. "She's the owner of the club."

"So what's the problem? You see something you like, you go after it. That's been the deal with you all along. She married?"

"Not that I know of. Didn't see any rings."

"Then I'm not getting it, Ray."

"I don't know, man...it's like I was saying, I guess I was wondering what it would be like to have just one woman, someone I could depend on from one day to the next and not want to forget her name as soon as possible."

Parker suddenly roared with laughter. "Man, this is serious. What did you do, fall and hit your head or something?" He took a swallow of beer to wash down his disbelief.

Now Ray felt like a fool. He knew he shouldn't have said anything to Parker. In Parker's mind, he would be forever young, forever single, forever on the prowl.

"I'll tell you what it would be like to be with the same woman day in and out—boring. Besides, you don't stay put long enough to stick to one woman," he added as if his last statement defined the mysteries of the universe.

Ray sat up, bracing his arms on his knees. As much as he hated to admit it, Parker was probably right. He'd spent the better part of his adult life roaming from one club, one city to the next. On a whole, it was a good life, an exciting one. There were never any two days that were the same. Maybe that was the trouble, what was finally getting to him. Some mornings not only didn't he know who was lying next to him, but even what city or hotel he was in. Unfortunately, it was the only life he knew, or understood. With no family ties to bind him, he was free. Yeah, right, free.

"Hey, man, you're probably right," Ray finally conceded. "Guess I was having a moment." He chuckled half-heartedly.

"That's more like it." Parker slapped Ray on the thigh. "Now can we get back to the game?" He pointed the remote and the roar from the stadium crowd filled the room. "Yes!" Parker shouted. "Giants, seven, Redskins, zip. My kinda game." He lifted his beer bottle in salute.

Ray decided to take Parker's advice on more than one level: his life and the game.

Usually after a Sunday football game, Ray and Parker drove into the Village to check out the jazz clubs, listen for any potential new talent that they should keep their ears on, or sometimes they'd sit in on a set and play with the band.

Parker was a master on keyboards, and many had compared him to Herbie Hancock, adding the fact that he looked like Herbie as well. Ray had lost count of how many times they'd used that ploy to get the best seats in the clubs or pick up women. However, Parker played only because it gave him entrée into another lifestyle. But not one in which he permanently wanted to live.

In Parker's real world he was an investment banker and a damned good one. Parker liked music and the attention that it brought. Ray loved it. Without it, he would be incomplete. Music defined who he was.

But tonight when Parker asked what time he wanted to head into the Village, Ray declined.

"You sure you're all right?" Parker asked.

"Yeah, yeah, I'm sure. I want to go home and practice this new piece for the band."

Parker frowned in suspicion, then shrugged. "Whatever you say."

Ray stood and slipped on his light brown leather jacket and grabbed his car keys from the coffee table, dumping them in his pocket.

Parker walked with him to the door. "I'll check you during the week."

Ray nodded. "Cool. Later." He jogged down the steps to the street.

Parker watched until Ray had pulled off in his black Maxima. Slowly, he shook his head and wondered what had gotten into his partner. It sounded like maturity, and all Parker could hope was that it wasn't catching.

Ray cruised for a bit, taking in the twilight sights of Brooklyn on the still warm fall evening. He wasn't sure why or how he found himself easing into the block of Soul to Soul. He knew the club wasn't open on Sunday, but he parked right out front anyway.

Sitting there, he wondered why he'd taken the job in the first place. The hours were more than he was used to putting in, and the money wasn't that great. But when he'd walked in for the first time, the atmosphere of the club called out to him. He easily sensed the warmth and friendship among everyone on the staff, especially the camaraderie of the band members. And Cole was a true gentleman. Yet, even after he'd accepted the spot, he'd had twinges of doubt. Until he'd seen Leone.

That's what his problem was. He knew it. There was something about Leone that had escalated the questions and doubts that had been rolling around in his head lately, even if she did keep him at a distance. But it was pretty obvious that Leone was Cole's woman. And as much as he might want to do otherwise, he never moved in on another man's woman.

FIVE

Every now and then, Leone would get the over-whelming urge to be alone in the club. Tonight was one of those nights. She needed to walk around in its emptiness, absorb the scents, imagine the sounds and remember that it was hers. It grounded her, reminded her that the sacrifices she'd made had been worth it. Somehow, being there validated her, rein-forced the fact that she could stand on her own, could fulfill her dreams, something Steven had insisted would never happen.

She straightened an autographed picture of Spike Lee with Denzel Washington, which had been taken when they were in town for the filming of Lee's last movie. She smiled. The music, the service and the food had made such an impression on Spike that whenever he wasn't at a Knicks game, he could be found with his wife at one of the back tables on a Friday night.

Leone walked toward the stage and stepped up. She looked upward at the spotlight, then closed her eyes, wondering what it would feel like to be the cen-ter of adoration, hear the rush of applause and shouts for more. How did it feel?

The sudden pounding on the glass door made her leap a good foot off the floor, her scream caught behind the hand that flew to her mouth. Wide-eyed and with her heart pounding, she peered in the direction of the entrance to see the outline of someone peering back at her.

Inhaling deeply, she jumped down off the stage and marched over to the door. Probably someone wanting to know if they were open, she fumed, trying to regulate her racing pulse.

She pressed her face to the glass and looked dead into the eyes of Ray Taylor, who was frowning at her as if she'd stolen the crown jewels. Her entire body went on full alert. A million thoughts tumbled through her head at once: the primary one being, did he see her making a fool of herself on stage?

Putting on her nonchalant expression, she twisted the locks on the door and cracked it open.

"Hi. What can I do for you, Ray?"

Ray peered over her shoulder trying to get a peek inside. "Everything okay?"

Leone put her hand on her hip, trying to regain some semblance of authority. "Of course. Why?"

His eyes narrowed. "I didn't know the club was open on Sunday."

"It's not. I just...I was here...doing... checking on the inventory." She cleared her throat and felt more ridiculous by the moment. This was her damned club and she could come in it whenever she pleased. So why did she feel like a bumbling idiot explaining this to Ray?

He stared at her a moment, then took another glance over her shoulder. "Well, if you're sure everything is all right," he said, his statement hanging like an unanswered question between them.

"Absolutely. Thanks."

Ray nodded and started to back off, then stopped. "You know, Leone, I'd feel a helluva lot better if you'd let me take a look inside...just to be sure."

Her brow wrinkled. "You're serious, aren't you?"

"Very."

With a huff, she stepped back and opened the door. "Come on in. See for yourself."

Ray eased by her and went inside. Slowly he perused the club, checking the kitchen, behind the bar, the storeroom and the office. Satisfied, he returned to the center of the club where Leone was seated at one of the tables, legs crossed and fingers tapping on the tabletop. She looked up when he approached.

"All clear?"

Ray grinned and her stomach see-sawed. "Yeah." He stuck his hands in his pockets. "I guess you must think I'm a bit nuts?"

Leone couldn't help smiling. "Not nuts...exactly. Just a bit over-zealous."

"If you'd been to as many spots as I have and seen as much, you'd understand my concern. I wouldn't have been able to forgive myself if somebody was in here and you had to play it off and I just walked away. It happens, you know."

Leone pursed her lips. "I guess you're right," she conceded, feeling suddenly foolish for being so short with him. "Thanks."

"Not a problem. Sorry if I took you away from what you were doing." He shrugged. "See you tomorrow." He began walking toward the door.

"What were you doing around this way?" Leone asked, stopping him in his tracks. She knew he lived in the Canarsie section of Brooklyn by the Pier. This was a bit out of the way simply to be passing along.

Ray turned. "I was hanging out with my man, Parker, watching the game." He came toward her. "Tell you the truth, I'm not sure what made me come over here. I looked up and I was on the block, so I stopped. Then I saw movement inside. At first I was going to call the cops." He chuckled. "Glad I didn't."

"You and me both."

"That would've made for an interesting Sunday evening."

"I can see it all now. Both of us being carted away with raincoats over our faces so we won't be recognized when the news van pulls up and the police haul us away."

"That would be a hoot. I can see you now trying to explain to your staff."

Leone shook her head, laughing. "It would definitely ruin my image."

Ray pulled up a seat. "Do you always come here when the place is closed?"

"Sometimes," she confessed.

"Want to remind yourself that it's real, huh?"

Leone angled her head to the side. "Yes. How did you know?"

Ray shrugged. "I do the same thing sometimes, pick up my sax and blow a few notes just to see if I can do it." He made little circles on the table with his finger.

"Why? You seem so confident on the stage... and off. Almost cocky," she added.

Ray inhaled deeply, trying to put his thoughts into words without coming off as if he were full of himself. He didn't want Leone to have that kind of impression about him. What she thought was suddenly important.

He tilted his head up toward the ceiling as he spoke. "When I get up on that stage, every nerve in my body feels like it's on fire, ready to leap out—or worse, strangle me. Sometimes I feel as if I can't breathe, that I'll get out there and forget everything I've ever learned. But when I come up to the mic or that spotlight hits me, something inside sparks with life and this rush, like a tidal wave roaring through me, pushes all the anxiety aside and it's just me and my sax playing like it was my first and last time. Everything just comes together." He lowered his gaze and looked at her, returning from the trip he'd taken.

"Wow," was all Leone could find to say. To watch Ray Taylor, you would never think that he would have an instant of doubt, a moment of vulnerability, she thought. Maybe he wasn't as shallow as he appeared.

Ray went back to making circles on the table with his fingertip.

Leone propped her chin up on her palm. "How did you get started? Were you forced into music lessons?" She laughed lightly.

"Not exactly. But it was a way to stay out of trouble. My math teacher got me involved with the school band to keep me from getting suspended."

"Oh." Her eyes widened in mock alarm. "So you were causing a stir even in your youth," she teased.

"One way or the other," he admitted, thinking back to his harrowing days as a gang member in D.C.

"But you must have liked it because you stuck with it."

"Yeah." He nodded. "I kind of dug it, especially when the girls—" He halted.

"Especially when the girls just drooled all over you, right?" Leone filled in.

Ray flashed an embarrassed smile and shrugged.

"It's apparent you haven't lost your touch."

"I don't know about all that. It's all an illusion. People see what they want to see." He looked directly at her.

Leone looked away, then stood. "Since we're here, would you like a drink—on the house?"

"Sure. Scotch and soda." He rose as well and followed her to the bar. "Let me do the honors." He stepped behind the bar. "What will you be having this evening, Ms. Weathers?"

The last thing she needed was to get lightheaded around Ray Taylor, but since she had made the suggestion...

"A rum and coke. Plenty of coke and plenty of ice."

He glanced up at her as he reached for the glasses beneath the counter. "Coming right up."

Leone slid onto one of the bar stools.

"So, tell me about you. How did you get into the nightclub business? Better yet, why? It can't be easy." He handed her the drink.

"Thanks." She took a sip and nodded her approval. "Why? Hmmm. Good question. I guess it came from watching so many old movies. It seemed like some of the greatest scenes took place in a nightclub," she said wistfully. "They always had this air of mystery about them, like anything could happen, anyone could walk in." She took another sip of her drink. "But of course, growing up to be a nightclub owner wasn't something my folks sent me to college to do. So I went into nursing."

"Nursing?"

"Yep. Twenty years."

Leone told him how much she loved nursing, but how she'd always dreamed of having a business of her own. She mentioned as quickly as possible her marriage to Steven and described in loving terms her daughter, Raven.

Ray leaned against the bar totally fascinated by Leone. He watched her eyes light up when she talked about her daughter, saw the lines of tension cross her face when she spoke of her marriage, heard the joy in her voice when she talked about the club and how proud she was of it.

He wanted to ask her about Cole. He wanted to know how old she was, especially since she had a seventeen year old daughter. He wanted to ask her about her childhood, her favorite book, movie, what she did in her spare time. He wanted to know what she thought about him. He wanted to know how serious it was between her and Cole Fleming. That question burned most of all.

But he asked none of that. Instead, he told her about his youth in D.C., the places he'd been and the clubs he'd played in. He shared with her his long-time friendship with Parker and his own passion for cooking and foreign movies.

As Leone listened, she realized with every passing minute that Ray Taylor was truly a complex man, an intelligent and sensitive man. He even had a wicked sense of humor. One by one all of her preconceived notions began to crumble and the restraining wall she'd built rocked on its foundation.

Ray paused briefly in the midst of his storytelling and smiled at her.

Leone knew in that instant that she was in big trouble.

SIX

Leone needed to get out of there. As much as she wanted to stay, as good as being with Ray made her feel, she knew she had to leave. But she couldn't seem to get her body to do anything other than surrender to the warm glow that Ray had thrown over her like a blanket.

As Ray drew to a close his tale of a college prank he and Parker had pulled on a girls' dorm, he glanced at Leone. She was quite pretty, he thought. Understated but pretty. There was a naturalness about her, a solid feeling that she exuded. There was no question in his mind that she was intelligent and determined. Otherwise she would have never been able to leave one career and start another one—and do it successfully. Leone had goals and a focus, qualities that were blatantly absent in most of the women he met. For the majority of them, their major concern was finding a man by any means necessary, and they'd go through all the hoops and whistles to get one. And then their true colors would show. Sure, he'd had his share of women, but one thing he always did was be up front. There was never a question dangling between him and any woman about what the extent of their relationship was to be.

Leone was unlike all the others. She had her own life. She didn't need him as a means to an end. If anything did jump off between them it would be because it was what they both wanted—more importantly, what Leone wanted.

The sound of her glass against the wood table drew him from his reverie.

"Hey, I didn't mean to keep you all this time running my mouth," Ray said, with a sheepish grin. "I know you must need to get home."

Leone checked her watch. She couldn't believe it. They'd been talking for nearly three hours. She looked toward the front door. It was pitch black outside. Night had definitely fallen. She pushed back from her seat and stood.

"I really do need to get moving. My daughter's going to be wondering—where's dinner?" she joked.

Ray stood. "You mean she's not going to be worried about where mom is?"

Leone twisted her mouth in a way that Ray found amusing. "Not hardly. She probably thinks I'm with Cole." Her heart suddenly thudded in her chest at the mention of Cole's name, and the spell that held her and Ray in place was broken.

"Cole's a lucky man."

She flashed him a brief smile. "I'm the lucky one."

They began to walk toward the door, while Leone checked lights and locks.

"How long have the two of you been together? If you don't mind my asking."

Leone punched in the alarm code. "About a year." She opened the door. "Hurry, hurry," she warned. "Or this thing will go off."

He walked to the other side of the door.

Leone came outside directly behind him and locked the door. Confident that all was secure, she turned to Ray. He stood barely a breath away.

"I had a nice time tonight. It's the first chance we've had to really talk, get to know each other," Ray said.

Leone felt as if all the available air was being sucked from her lungs. She was close enough to him to see the hairline scar that ran across his right eyebrow and the brown rim that circled his eyes.

She swallowed. "I had a good time too, but I—"

"I know, you have to get home." He looked around. "Where's your car?"

"I walked. I only live a few blocks away."

"I'll drive you. It's late."

"No, really—"

"I insist. Come on. I'm parked right here."

Being alone with him in the club was one thing, in close quarters inside his car was another story, she worried.

Ray saw her uncertainty, the doubt that made her twist her lips in thought.

"I promise you, I'll keep both hands on the wheel," he said laughing.

Leone bit back a smile. "Well, in that case—okay."

She slid into the sleek car seat and immediately put on her belt, positioning herself as close to the passenger door as possible. Quickly, she folded her hands on her lap as Ray hopped in.

The air suddenly became close and tight, Leone realized. The masculine scent of Ray assaulted her senses. She could feel his body heat as surely as if he stroked her with it. She crossed her legs to stem the smoldering fire.

"Where to?" He stuck the key in the ignition and the Maxima hummed like a vibrator beneath them.

"Greene and Clinton."

Ray snatched a glance at her before pulling away from the curb. "You really do live close. By the time the car warms up good, you'll be home."

"I tried to tell you," she said in the same, 'I told-you-so' tone she used with Raven when her daughter would finally concede that her mother knew what she was talking about.

Ray grumbled something in his throat before switching the radio station to CD 101.9, the local jazz station. Nancy Wilson's voice filled the space.

Majestic brownstones, refurbished to their original glory, proudly stood side-by-side on the tree-lined streets. No more than twenty years earlier, this entire area of Brooklyn had been a "runaway" zone—everyone who lived there wanted to run away from the crime and decay. Somehow word got out that there was prime property falling by the wayside and money and loans that were previously unavailable slowly began to materialize. Now, homes that at one time couldn't be given away, are some of the most highly priced, desirable properties in the borough.

"How long have you lived in the area?" Ray asked, making a right onto Clinton Avenue.

Leone couldn't help noticing the way his body became one with the car, moving in perfect harmony. She swallowed. "We moved out here from Queens when my ex-husband was assigned to manage part of the construction of Metrotech."

"Really. That's the collection of businesses and corporate offices further downtown, right?"

"Yes."

"Your husband—"

"Ex," she quickly corrected.

"Ex...is a builder?"

"Yep. Pretty good at it, too." She adjusted her purse on her lap and glanced out her window.

"He, uh, still around?"

Leone cut her eyes in his direction. Ray stared straight ahead.

"Make a right at the next corner." She paused another beat. "He's in North Carolina last I heard."

"Oh."

Leone watched the lines of tension ease from around his eyes and the corners of his mouth. The fierce grip he had on the steering wheel lessened. She smiled to herself and suddenly felt bold.

"Where's your wife, or significant other?"

"Don't have one," he answered without blinking an eye.

"Intentional or circumstantial?"

He glanced briefly in her direction. "A little of both."

"I'm three houses from the corner. On your left." She'd heard his response, but felt it best not to pursue it. It would be so easy to fall into a comfortable banter with him, exchange information, pasts, ideas...kisses. That was the problem. "Thanks a lot. I'm right here."

Ray eased to the curb and cut the engine. When Leone turned to say goodnight, she caught him peering up at the darkened windows of her building.

"You need me to go up with you? Check everything out?"

This time she did laugh. "No. But thanks, anyway." She unbuckled her belt. 'I'll be fine. Scout's honor."

His left eyebrow rose in question. "Hmm. If you say so. But you'll have to ignore me while I sit here and make sure you get inside safely."

"You're really quite a gentleman," she said, her tone sounding as if she'd grasped a new realization.

"Why is that so hard to believe—about me?"

The bottomless level that his voice had reached settled in the center of Leone's stomach and radiated like sunbeams through her body. A trickle of perspiration wiggled its way down her spine.

She swallowed. "It's just...nice to know, I suppose. Finding men that go that extra distance is a treat."

Ray unfastened his belt and angled his body toward her. Leone's belly fluttered, her body tensed.

"There's probably a lot of things about me that would surprise you." His gaze danced over her face, stopped briefly at the pulse in her throat, then returned to rest on her eyes.

"Like what?" She sounded almost breathless to her own ears and the realization unnerved her even more.

He raised his arm and for an instant, Leone knew he was going to touch her. She wanted him to. Instead, he stretched his arm along the back of the headrest, which was ultimately worse. The proximity of his hand to the exposed flesh of her neck was more tantalizing than if he'd kissed her.

The corner of his mouth curved in a tempting, almost boyish grin.

"Besides being a gentleman, I—"

The loud rapping on the passenger window made Leone gasp with fear. Startled eyes snapped toward the sound of the intrusion. Staring her in the face was Raven.

Leone quickly shut her eyes and inhaled. "Twice in one day," she mumbled.

"Who's that?"

"My daughter," she said, depressing the diagramed button to lower the window.

"Hi, Ma." Raven greeted, staring at Ray and ignoring her mother.

"Are you just getting home?" Leone questioned, knowing full well that the answer was obvious.

"Uh huh. Hi, I'm Raven." She brazenly introduced herself when it seemed that her mother had no intention of crossing that bridge.

"Ray Taylor. I work at the club."

"Really!" she chirped in the high pitch that only teen girls can reach.

Ray chuckled. "Really."

Raven poked her mother in the shoulder. "You didn't tell me."

Leone struggled to maintain her calm demeanor. "Didn't think I had to." She turned to Ray. "Thanks for the lift, Ray. I'll see you tomorrow." She opened the door and Raven leaped back to avoid getting knocked down.

"What's wrong with you?" Raven hissed from between her teeth. Leone ignored her.

Ray lowered his head to better see the departure of his riding companion. "Yeah, see ya. Nice meeting you, Raven."

"You, too," she replied, a bit too sweetly for Leone's tastes.

"Let's go, Raven. You should have been home a half hour ago. Tomorrow's a school day," Leone continued to fuss, thankful for the distraction.

"M—a," she complained before grudgingly trailing behind her mother.

Leone ignored her and marched up the steps to the glass and wood front door. All the while she was keenly aware that Ray hadn't moved from his sentinel position in front of her door. She stuck the key in the lock and quickly stepped inside, shutting the door and Ray firmly behind her.

Ray watched as the house came to illuminated life. Hmm. He'd seen Leone the businesswoman, Leone the mother and disciplinarian. He was impressed with what he saw and wondered what Leone the woman was like.

SEVEN

"He is fine," Raven announced, emphasizing each word. She dropped her purse on the kitchen counter.

"Instead of worrying about who's fine and who isn't, you need to get yourself together for school tomorrow." Leone pulled open the refrigerator door and removed a can of soda. The telltale sound of fizz shortly followed and she took a short, cool swallow.

"What is wrong with you?" Raven asked in that sing-song cadence that belied the challenge in her voice.

Leone cut her eyes in her daughter's direction.

"Nothing."

"Really?"

"Yes. Really."

Raven stared at her mother, trying to find a way around the barrier. "Where's Cole?" Her tone became accusatory. "How come I haven't seen him lately?"

"Cole is wherever he is. People do get busy, Raven."

"Too busy to see me? He always comes to see me. He hasn't even called. Did you run him away, too?"

Leone flashed her a warning look. Raven was treading on dangerous ground, and Leone knew if she didn't nip this in the bud, the conversation would rapidly segue to her ex-husband, Steven. And he was a topic she refused to discuss.

She pressed her palm to her forehead and spoke through tight lips. "Raven—please—go see about your clothes for tomorrow, pack your books and take your shower."

"Fine. Every time I want to talk about something, it's a problem." She snatched her bag from the counter and stomped up the stairs to her bedroom.

An instant later, the house rocked in its hinges with the inevitable slamming of Raven's bedroom door.

Leone shut her eyes, inhaling deeply. Like all the other storms before, this one would pass as well. She opened an overhead cabinet and extracted a teacup. The caffeine in the soda would only make her more agitated than she already was. She rifled around in the cabinet for her box of chamomile tea, and put a pot of water on to boil.

Even though Raven was old enough to understand that her parents' marriage wasn't working, there were days like this one that she would lash out at being "a statistic," Leone thought, watching the water begin to bubble in the pot.

Cole was the only man she'd allowed into her life since her divorce from Steven. And Raven, although tenuous at first, slowly formed a bond with him that she'd never had with her own father. At times Raven seemed closer to Cole than to her. According to Antoinette, it was Raven's need to have a positive male role model that helped seal the bond.

Cole loved Raven, and thought of her as the daughter he never had, Leone reflected, pouring the hot water over the tea bag. The three of them made a great team, and for the most part she was happy. Yet, for the life of her, she couldn't understand her growing restlessness, her dissatisfaction. Even more disturbing was the steady beat of sensory arousal whenever she thought of or saw Ray Taylor.

Why? Why? Why? she questioned, taking a sip of her tea. But even as she posed the silent question, she knew that the answer rested inside herself.

Cole watched the black Maxima pull away from the curb and something deep inside of him twisted like wet clothes being wrung dry.

One by one the lights in the house filled the windows. He should get out of his car, cross the street and ring Leone's bell as he'd intended to do in the first place, until he saw her pull up with Ray.

He turned the key in the ignition, switched on his headlights and pulled away. He didn't want to see the lies in her eyes, or hear them from her lips.

EIGHT

Cole slowly walked into his Manhattan co-op and switched on the light. He tossed his car keys onto the small circular table in the short foyer and went straight to the mini-bar.

He didn't usually drink alone, but felt as if he needed one now. He poured some Scotch over ice and stretched out on the couch, taking a long swallow. The amber liquid burned all the way down and settled in the pit of his belly. Yet, it couldn't melt the chill that had settled there.

What was happening between him and Leone? Where had their relationship taken a wrong turn?

He leaned his head back against the cushions and closed his eyes.

They'd met when she'd put an ad in Backstage Magazine just before she opened the club, looking for a small band.

At first he thought about ignoring it. He knew the difficulty of working with folks who were just starting out. He'd been through enough "start up" operations and wanted something solid. But on the other hand, he'd grown weary of the short stints at one club or the other, never sure from week to week where the next check was coming from. The saving grace for him was that he had no family to concern himself with. The same couldn't be said for the rest of the band members, and he felt responsible for that, responsible for them. They all worked other jobs to make ends meet, but music was their first love. If a permanent gig could be set up, they'd give up their day jobs in a heartbeat.

So, finally he called and set up a meeting for the following afternoon. He wasn't sure what he expected, but it certainly wasn't Leone Williams.

"We can talk in the office," Leone said as she led him through what would become Soul to Soul once the construction was completed.

Cole took in the surroundings, the solidness of the structure, which had once been an antique shop, and marveled at what was being done with the place.

The vastness of the central room was being totally reconfigured with several pillars and a drop ceiling with recessed track lighting around the perimeter.

The old floor had been completely ripped out and replaced with a black marble-like surface except for the dance area which was a hi-gloss parquet. Mirrors lined one wall, giving the illusion of even more space. The once dreary walls were being painted in a soft teal with a deeper teal molding.

"Please excuse the mess," she said, laughing lightly. "We still have a way to go before everything is the way I want it."

"It looks like it's going to be great," he answered, stepping around a crate of framed artwork. "You've put a lot into this place. I remember it being dark and gloomy and crammed with furniture."

She turned to him and flashed the most exquisite smile he'd ever seen. "You've been here before?" Her eyes sparkled.

"Yeah, a few years ago. I was searching for an old rollback desk and a friend of mine told me about this place." He glanced around again.

"Changed a bit," she teased.

"I'd say so. And for the better."

Leone opened the door to the office. "Welcome to operation central." She extended her hand to wave him inside.

Cole stepped into the sparse room. There was one age-old desk and two wooden chairs that looked as if they'd been left behind by the last tenants. It quickly reminded him of those sinister back rooms from the old black and white movies. But when Leone stepped in and closed the door behind her, everything became colorized and Cole was instantly taken aback by the sudden rush that overtook him.

Leone came around the desk and sat down. "Please, sit."

Cole took the lone available seat. "Looks like you have your hands full, Ms. Weathers." He crossed his right ankle over his left knee.

"It's hectic, crazed and totally insane, but I'm loving every minute. If everything stays on schedule, I should be ready to open in a month." She cleared her throat and leaned slightly forward. "So, tell me a little about yourself and what you've done."

"What haven't I done?" he said with a short laugh. "I guess it goes all the way back to high school. My folks insisted that I take piano lessons, which, of course, I hated. But in my junior year a friend of my father wanted to put a band together. I tried out and the rest is history. I did local stuff until I got out of school. By then I had the bug and wanted my own band." The corner of his mouth curved upward. "Not too good at taking orders and playing other people's music. Started writing my own and recruiting the band."

"How long has your band been together?"

"About fifteen years, give or take a few personnel changes."

Leone nodded. "When do you think you could come in so I can hear you?"

"Whenever you're ready."

"How about Friday evening, around eight."

"Sounds good."

Leone stood. "So, we'll meet on Friday and take it from there." She extended her hand. "Thank you for coming."

The first thing he thought was how soft, almost fragile her hand was. Yet Leone Weathers was anything but fragile. Reluctantly he released her hand. "My pleasure."

He followed her to the door. "Are you taking on this whole project yourself?"

"Pretty much. Everyone thinks I'm crazy, but it's what I want. I want to see it work out."

There was something in her voice, more than determination. She had something to prove to herself and he wondered what it was. "I'm sure it will," he said finally.

They reached the front door and faced each other. When she looked up at him, he felt that rush again, that heat in the center of his stomach.

"Listen, uh, if there's anything I can help you with, don't hesitate to ask. Whether I get the job or not, the offer is still good."

"I just might take you up on that, Mr. Fleming."

"See you on Friday."

"Eight o'clock."

As promised, Cole arrived with the band on Friday
night, and before they'd finished the third number
Leone said they had the job if they wanted it.

"I can't pay much to start," she said when she and
Cole had retreated to her office. "But the pay is guar-
anteed and steady."

"I'll talk it over with the guys, but I don't think it'll
be a problem."

"Great. I'll have the contract ready for you to sign
in the next couple of days. Do you want to come and
pick it up or should I mail it to your home?"

Mailing it would save him a drive, but coming to
pick it up would give him the chance to see her again.

Since their first meeting, Leone had dominated his
thoughts. He'd tried to conceive of all types of reasons
to call her, just to hear her voice, but had decided
against it. There was no point in making a fool of
himself. Besides, a woman as lovely and together as
Leone surely had a man of her own. But if she did,
where was he?

"I can drop by and pick it up. Give me a call when
it's ready."

"I'll do that."

Her face lit up when she smiled. "Welcome
aboard."

"I have a feeling it's going to be a great ride.
Maybe, if you're not busy, we can celebrate after we
get all the paperwork out of the way."

She tilted her head a bit to the side. "I'd like that.
What did you have in mind?"

Even though he'd hoped she'd say yes, the actuality caught him off guard. This woman didn't play games.

"Let me surprise you," he said, recovering quickly.

"I like surprises."

"Then I'll have to make it a good one. See you in a couple of days."

"I'm looking forward to it—Cole."

And so it began.

NINE

Cole intended to make that first night memorable. Every time Leone thought about one of the great evenings of her life, he wanted her to think of him.

He'd gotten tickets for a midnight cruise around Manhattan Island, complete with dinner and dancing under the stars. The evening was magical. They ate lobster and drank champagne amidst a warm sea breeze and the gentle undulations of waves beneath them. From there it was a series of romantic interludes: talks long into the night, drives upstate for middle-of-the-week picnics. And when they made love for the very first time, it left him weak with an unnamed joy.

Maybe that was when he realized he was falling in love with Leone. But that couldn't be, he reasoned. He was a rational man. He thought things through logically. But when it came to Leone, nothing made sense.

It was the little things she did: a gentle touch or a look, like slipping loving notes into his shirt pockets, or giving him a massage, right in the office.

The first six months of their relationship was like being a kid again. He was in love. Really in love. And it scared him. The last time he'd turned his heart over to someone, he'd been burned. He still carried the scars of Tara Bentley.

Humph. Tara. She was pretty, smart, sexy, driven by her career as a television producer and totally self-absorbed. Tara gave the illusion of caring about others. She could even say the words "I love you," without flinching. But Cole found out the hard way that the only person Tara loved was herself and what someone else could do for her.

"I'm getting married," Tara had calmly announced as they lay in bed together. Cole's body still vibrated from the lovemaking session they'd just concluded.

He chuckled deep in his throat. "I didn't know we'd set a date, babe." He stroked her bare back.

Tara stretched her long, tan legs toward the ceiling, then lowered them to the damp sheets.

"Not to you, silly." She eased off the bed and paraded her perfect body toward the chair where she'd tossed her clothes.

For an instant his mind went blank. Nothing was there. He saw everything around him, but couldn't process the information. Then that sudden rush of realization, that free-fall feeling in your belly pushed its way upward, trapping his breath in his throat, and wouldn't let go.

Fear of choking forced the words out. "What are you talking about?" It was all he could think coherently to ask.

She wouldn't look at him as she put one foot, then the other, through the openings in her panties and wiggled them in place.

"Paul and I are getting married."

Cole blinked as if smacked. All he could see in that instant was the helpless look on his father's face when his mom took the kids and walked out, and that sick sensation of loss that he, himself, felt and was never able to fill. He shook his head, then suddenly jumped up and crossed the room. He grabbed Tara by the arms and spun her around.

"What the fuck are you saying to me? Don't play." His eyes narrowed to two single slits. He could feel the pull in his chest as his heart banged viciously.

She glared down at his hands. "You're hurting me," she said matter-of-factly. "I'm marrying Paul Howell in two weeks. I thought you should know. She looked into his eyes as innocently as if she'd just relayed the forecast for a sunny, cloudless day.

He wanted to hurt her, knock the smug, self-satisfied look off her face. Most of all he wanted to make her hurt the way he was hurting now. But standing there, staring into her soulless eyes, he understood as never before that making Tara feel anything was beyond anyone's ability.

He pushed her away from him and laughed, a deep belly laugh that filled the bedroom and the one beyond. "Think you can get dressed a little faster? I have some music I want to work on." He shook his head trying to catch his breath and pulled on his shorts.

Tara pulled her top over her braless torso and looked at him in stunned disbelief. "Cole, I'm not kidding. What we had was nice. But it could never go anywhere."

"Of course not." He crossed the room to the dresser. "Don't forget your purse."

"You hop from one job to the next. All you ever talk about is music and that rag-tag band of yours." Her voice rose in confrontation. "What can you offer me? Huh? What?"

Cole ignored her as he flipped through his phone book. He needed something to do with his hands to keep them from wrapping around her neck.

"You barely make enough money to pay your rent," she said, needing to penetrate this unfamiliar wall he'd erected. She fastened her skirt and stepped into her pumps.

His mother had spat those same words to his father as she walked out the door. Heat rushed to his head and took on a life of its own as it throbbed.

"It was good, Cole," she flung at him in a last ditch effort. "But it's not what I want."

He picked up the phone. "Oh, just pull the door behind you," he said over his shoulder. "And don't forget to leave the keys on the kitchen table."

Tara glared at him one last time, snatched up her purse and stormed out.

That was nearly ten years ago. Yet, even now, the thought of that night made him feel worthless and used. It made him wary and uncertain. Anger and frustration would fill him and he'd pick up a drink. He did that just about everyday until he saw the ad in the paper and met Leone.

From that first day, his life began to change. He found his humanity again, his self-esteem. And it was because of Leone—her kindness, her love, her acceptance of who he was began to heal him. He started to trust again—love again.

Cole blinked and looked around his neat, contemporarily furnished apartment. It had gone through some major overhauling since he'd started working at

Soul to Soul. His drink had gone flat. He poured it out and refreshed it.

Now, he was right back where he started ten years ago. He'd opened himself up, turned over his emotions, and it was happening again. Again.

Suddenly he hurled the glass against the wall. It splintered and fell in a pile of sparkling rubble, while tears of Scotch streaked down the white surface.

He wouldn't go down that road. Not this time.

TEN

The following morning, Raven barely spoke to her mother before leaving for school. There was a near audible grunt, which could have meant hello or goodbye, depending on which way Raven was going.

Leone pushed her scrambled eggs around on her plate, then stared into her coffee cup.

Last night, if Raven hadn't walked up when she did—she didn't want to think about it. But what truly unnerved her was that she would have let Ray kiss her. She wanted him to. That same exhilaration that you experience when you play tag and you can feel the kid who's "it" right on your heels. And you run and run, excited and scared at the same time.

That's the way she'd felt in the car, like something unseen, untapped was racing behind her, ready to catch her.

There was something mysterious, inaccessible about Ray Taylor. For all his affability, warm smile and good looks, he was undefined, yet to be discovered. That was the attraction, the challenge.

Ray awakened the core of her, the Leone who'd never been allowed to "go off the block," "attend the public school," "wear lipstick or mini skirts," "date before high school graduation." Ray represented "yes you can."

Leone took a sip of her cool coffee and stared out the kitchen window that looked upon a small, untended backyard. Steven had promised to cement part of it and trim the unruly trees so that they could use it in the summer. Never happened. And she refused to do it. She knew it was childish, but it was one of the few ways to show her displeasure. What had been the pattern during their marriage was for Leone to always pick up where Steven left off—from paying the bills to repairs on the house to disciplining Raven. The list went on. She supposed it was just easier that way; easier not to complain, not to make an issue, not to nag. She'd been conditioned to follow protocol. Why would her marriage be any different?

Leaving her job of twenty years, divorcing Steven and finally opening the club had all been acts of long overdue rebellion. She knew that. It had been terrifying and everyday she knew she'd gone completely crazy. And at the same time she felt rejuvenated as if she'd been asleep and just going through the motions for most of her life.

Meeting and settling into a relationship with Cole had been the equivalent of reaching for a life preserver after you've dived off the side of the ship and realize you can't swim. He was safe, secure, the calm during the storm of change in her life—what she needed—what she'd been conditioned to be accustomed to—the status quo.

Now she felt torn. Torn between the Leone who would never jump ship and the one who'd learned how to swim.

Ray had gotten up at first light, tossed some water on his face, brushed his teeth and donned his jogging clothes—nothing fancy—just a ragged pair of navy blue sweatpants and a cut-off T-shirt.

He stood on his front porch and looked out across the water. The air was crisp, sharp like a paper's edge when he stepped outside, pulling in a lungful of air. The blue-green waves rolled gently, one massaging the other. In the distance, he spotted several small pleasure boats out for an early morning sail.

Parker had been instrumental in securing the house for him. With his transient lifestyle and sporadic, though bountiful, financial situation, the bank was reluctant to approve the mortgage. Parker, "Mr. Negotiator," was somehow able to convince the bank to give Ray the loan. It wasn't until later that Ray discovered Parker had used his own home as collateral.

Ray inhaled deeply of the sea-touched air. This was the first place he'd called home since he left his folks and went to college. Most of his adult life had been moving from one city to the next. One kitchenette or studio to another. And as much as Parker might profess his love for the prowl and new adventures, he was probably the most settled, stable guy Ray knew. Parker might run a good game, but at the heart of it he was a seriously practical man. He owned his house, his car, had a huge stash in the bank and wore a suit and tie five days a week.

Ray trotted out of the cul-de-sac of houses and onto the unpaved road, jogging along the shoreline.

At times, especially lately, he envied Parker, envied him more than he'd ever admit. The funny thing was, as quiet as it was kept, Parker felt the same way about him. The grass is always greener on the other side, he mused, catching sight of a sailboat on the horizon.

But Parker was the kind of guy a woman settled down with, made a life with—even though he'd never get Parker to agree.

He on the other hand could always fill "the temp" position. Do it well for a little while, just not forever. For the most part it was fine. It worked with the kind of life he'd been living. But more and more, he realized that what had always been was no longer enough. He gazed out toward a grassy patch shaded by an overhanging tree and noticed an embracing couple simply sitting together enjoying the view.

That's what he wanted. Right there.

An image of Leone's face, the expectation in her eyes last night, materialized before him and that tightness in his chest took hold again.

That's who he wanted. But she belonged to someone else.

ELEVEN

"What are you doing after work today?" Leone asked, hugging the phone between her shoulder and her left ear, as she polished her toes a pearly peach. She knew Antoinette usually finished her day anywhere between two and three in the afternoon. But sometimes, she'd get a last minute call for a job that could run well into the night. She hoped today wouldn't be one of them.

Antoinette's slim fingers quickly typed in a string of programming commands on the computer. She'd gone into computer programming and repair about eight years earlier and loved it. Between the incredible pay, a flex schedule, access to a company car, frequent flyer miles for all the trips she had to take, she couldn't ask for more. Not to mention all of the eligible men.

"This is where the guys are, Lee," she'd said when she entered the training program. "Short, tall, dark, light, fat, thin. They all have brains and will have bucks."

"Been there, done that."

"Let's do it again and again," Antoinette sang off-key.

Now she was head of the programming division and free-lanced for major companies across the country. She'd set up Leone's computer system at the club and it had been a management lifesaver.

"So, what are you doing later?" Leone asked again.

"Sorry, drifted for a minute. Can't seem to get this damned system to run right." She sucked her teeth in disgust. "I don't have any plans. What's up?"

Leone sighed. "Just thought you could hang out for a while before I went to work."

"Sure. Where?"

"Can you come by the house?"

"This doesn't sound like a girls' night out to me."

"I just want some quiet time, that's all."

"Hmm. Okay. I'm sure you'll give me the scoop later. I'll come if you promise to fix the breaded chicken breasts for dinner."

"Nettie," Leone whined.

"Then I ain't comin'."

"All right, all right. Six o'clock. Don't be late."

"Yes, ma'am."

Leone hung up the phone and smiled. Antoinette had some wild ideas about love and life, but she had a good ear, and what she needed right now was someone to listen to all the scattered thoughts that were running rampant in her head.

"Where's Raven?" Antoinette asked later that evening as she swiped a celery stick from the salad bowl.

"Sequestered in her room." Leone checked the chicken in the oven.

Antoinette flicked an eyebrow at the sarcastic tone. "Why is that?"

"We had words last night and she apparently hasn't gotten over it yet."

The oven door banged shut. Leone tossed the pot holder on the counter and grabbed her glass of iced tea.

"You and Raven have been doing great lately. She's keeping up her grades, has a good group of friends, does her thing around the house. What happened?"

Leone's gaze bounced around the kitchen as if the answers could be found in one of the many wood cabinets. She released a sigh and lowered herself onto a stool opposite Antoinette.

"I was with Ray last night," she began, filling Antoinette in on all the details up to when Raven tapped on the window.

Antoinette stared at Leone's averted profile. "It sounds to me that you felt guilty—for whatever reason—and took it out on Raven," she said pragmatically.

"Guilty about what?"

"You tell me."

Leone huffed and sipped her drink. "There's nothing to tell. Nothing went on."

"So then why take it out on Raven?"

"She was being rude and out of place," Leone snapped.

"Raven was being seventeen." Antoinette stretched her hand across the table and covered Leone's. "Let's cut through all the bull, Lee. We've been friends too long to play games. The bottom line is, you're confused about your feelings for this guy, don't know what to do about them, and Raven was the most accessible target for venting your frustration."

Leone remained silent.

"Am I right?"

"I hate it when you're right," Leone conceded and rolled her eyes.

"Yeah, I know. So, what's going on, girl? You're making yourself crazy."

"A part of me wants to see what it would be like with Ray. Take a chance, you know. I see him with the other women in the club. I know I can't compete with that. And at the same time when I see all those young girls all over him, it really ticks me off, because it's not me. I don't know what it is about Ray Taylor that sets my blood boiling. Maybe it's just the challenge, the desire to be noticed, to not be looked at as a woman moving out of her forties. But at the same time, I don't want to hurt Cole. He doesn't deserve that. He's been good to me and for me. I mean, I've only known Ray for a little more than two months. And we never really talked until last night. I've been working real hard to stay away from him. But when we finally did talk, I began to see that he's nothing like I thought." She lowered her head. "Which only makes things worse."

"Listen, maybe I was jumping the gun the last time we talked about this. It's not up to me to tell you to drop your man for some other guy. You know me, talk faster than I can think sometimes. Cole is a damned good man. Maybe this Ray guy is, too. Only you know who and what is right for you, Lee."

"It wasn't anything you said. It's me. I'm at a crossroads in my life. If I settle down again, like Cole wants, I need to be absolutely sure. I don't want to wake up in six months after saying 'I do' and wonder 'what if.'"

"Hey, I know what you mean. That would be the worse mistake you could make. Maybe the whole notion of getting married again has you running scared. Scared enough that you've started talking yourself out of your relationship with Cole, finding things wrong that aren't. Maybe what you need is a short break, give yourself some time and space to think."

"I've been thinking the same thing. A break may be just what I need."

TWELVE

When Leone arrived at the club later that day, the band was on stage going over a new number. Cole's back was turned to her while he gave out instructions about how he wanted each section played.

He never ceased to amaze her, she mused, a soft smile of pride softening her mouth. He was not only an incredible musician, but a wonderful manager. The guys in the band practically worshipped him. He was always fair and open-minded and was eager to give each of them a shot at a solo. He'd even helped them compose some of their own pieces. Yeah, she was lucky to have a man like Cole Fleming, and she was going to remind him of that—tonight. She didn't need a break, she'd decided after a long talk with her heart. What she needed was to start acting like a grown woman, get her love life back on track and stop thinking like a college coed. Cole was her man. Period. Simple as that. She leaned against a pillar and watched him do his thing. She smiled. Yeah, her man.

"Come in slow and easy, Ray, right above Zach's bass," Cole guided. "Think of yourself as the ship sailing across the water. We're the water, Ray," he coaxed. "Take us sailing."

Cole hit the first chords on the piano and one by one the rest of the band joined in.

Ray nodded, closed his eyes and brought the sax to his lips, the plaintive cry rolling on along the crest of the waves.

The music rippled through Leone, scurried along her spine, and she trembled as if some erotic zone had been entered and caressed. Music always had the power to do that to her, reach her somehow. It was, beyond his charm, one of the things that had attracted her to Cole. The more she heard him play and experienced the deep-seated passion he had for his craft, the more enchanted she became. Then, getting to know Cole the man away from the music was even more enlightening.

She supposed it really hit her just how good a man he was when he met Raven for the first time.

She'd decided that since it was no longer hush-hush around the club about their relationship, it was time she introduced "her man" to her daughter.

Leone had been reluctant at first, partly out of fear that Raven would hate him simply because he wasn't her father, or turn on her because there was now someone in her life besides Raven.

"Listen, babe," Cole had said one late night at his apartment. "I've never been the kind of man who sneaks around, and that's what this feels like to me." He eased closer on the couch, put his arm around her rigid shoulders and pulled her near. "I don't want to be the family secret. I think we're great together, and I want to see how far things can go with us. But I won't commit myself to the program if we can't be up front with your daughter. I know once we meet and she sees how much I care about you, it will be fine."

Leone glanced up at him from the corner of her eye. She knew he was right, but...

"Cole," she blew out. "It's just that I've never, I mean I haven't dated anyone since my divorce." There, she'd said it—finally.

"No one?" he asked incredulously.

She shook her head. "Not a soul." She waited a beat, collected her thoughts. "So, I have no clue as to how Raven will react. Although things were strained in the household, she adored her father."

"Most girls do."

"But you understand what I'm saying, right?"

"Sure. You don't want Raven to think I'm trying to take her father's place."

She nodded slowly.

"I couldn't, Lee. And I wouldn't want to. There isn't anything I could do in this lifetime to be able to step into your ex-husband's shoes. No matter what I did, the shoes would never fit. All I can be is who I am. And be the best I can at it. I don't expect Raven to love me on sight, but I tend to grow on people." He gently tickled her side. She giggled. "Besides, we'll never know if we don't give it a shot."

She released a short breath. "I guess you're right." She turned fully toward him, needing to see assurance in his dark eyes.

"It'll be all right," he said, reading her thoughts as he was prone to do. He stroked her hair, then tucked it behind her ears. "Raven couldn't really believe that you've given up living, given up your womanhood because your husband is no longer in your life."

She pursed her lips.

"It might help Raven to see that her mom is still loveable, still beautiful," he added, his voice dropping to a caress. He tilted her chin upward with the tip of his finger. "And very desirable," he murmured before bringing his mouth to hers.

It was a sweet sensation, Leone thought, letting her lids slide shut and easing into the secure comfort of Cole's embrace. He made her feel good from the inside out. Cole had a natural way of making her believe that everything would be all right, no matter what. He could make love to her body as well as her mind.

Neither of them was as young as they once were, but their loving was strong, filled not only with passion, but the maturity of experience. They understood the act of pleasuring each other, the power of the slow hand and hot spring words.

They fit each other physically and mentally. They accepted the extra pounds, the touches of gray, the skin that was smooth, if not workout firm. It was good. It was easy.

Yet for all the assertions Cole made that everything would be fine, it didn't keep Leone's stomach from running an unwinable marathon that fateful Sunday afternoon.

She'd spent the entire morning cleaning, dusting, organizing and cooking. She'd broken out some of her favorite cookbooks and had prepared a head-spinning array of exotic platters from French finger foods to West Indian delicacies.

Every time a door closed, the phone rang or Raven called her name, she leaped from the inside out. She felt the way she did when she was preparing for her first solo date and knew her father and mother would

interrogate her new beau and embarrass her the way
they always did around her friends. She was so nervous waiting to be picked up that she'd thrown up and
developed a raging headache. She never thought she'd
feel like that again—until now.

By the time four o'clock rolled around—the time
she'd invited Cole—she was on the verge of tossing
down some Pepto Bismol.

She checked every room, one last time. Turning
from fluffing the couch pillows, she gasped at finding
Raven standing behind her.

"Who is this dude, anyway—the President's half
brother?" Raven suspiciously scanned the counter as
she sauntered into the kitchen. It was lined from one
end to the other with food.

"No, smarty. He's just a friend. I told you that,"
Leone said entering the kitchen.

"He's the band leader, right?"

"Yes."

Raven picked up a buffalo wing and took a bite.

"Any other questions?"

Raven shrugged. "I don't have to hang around all
afternoon do I? Ron asked me to go to the movies
later."

Leone arched a brow. "I suppose it'll be all right.
He has to come and pick you up and you need to be
home by eleven."

"But, Ma, it's summertime," she whined.

"Raven, I—"

The doorbell rang, cutting her off. She quickly
wiped her hands on a towel and headed for the door.
"Midnight," she tossed over her shoulder.

Whatever anxiety she'd harbored about Raven's
reaction to Cole quickly dissolved.

After the initial introductions, Cole and Raven launched into a quick and easy banter about music, music videos, rap groups she'd never heard of, the latest singing sensations, books, movies, cars, clothes.

Cole was "up" on everything it seemed, Leone mused as she mixed the salad and listened to their laughter from the living room. She couldn't remember the last time she and Raven talked for more than twenty minutes without getting into a conflict about something. She tossed the salad a bit faster. Humph.

Raven popped up behind her and snatched a carrot from the bowl. "He's cool, Ma." She grinned. "And he even knows Maxwell! Can you believe it?" Maxwell, this R&B generation's heir apparent to the late Marvin Gaye, was, according to Raven, the cousin of a friend's ex-in-law. Go figure.

"That's great. I'm glad you two are getting along. Would you take the tray of sandwiches inside for me and ask Cole if he wants anything to drink?"

"He says he likes Coke with lemon." She spun away toward the refrigerator. "I'll fix it."

Leone blinked. Who was this child in front of her and what did they do with her real daughter? She shook her head in amazement.

And that's how it always was between Raven and Cole. He'd drop by and they'd talk for hours. He'd slip extra money in her pocket when she'd spent her allowance. He'd drive her and her friends to the mall without complaint. Pick her and Ron up from a date. He even got along with Ron, who she'd always believed couldn't put three whole sentences together. And she was certain Raven shared secrets with Cole that she wouldn't dare tell her.

Yes, Cole Fleming had eased into their lives, like the missing piece of a puzzle, she thought, as the music in the club came to a climactic finish.

Leone blinked and the past receded. A quiet sense of peace moved slowly through her. She had a good thing with Cole, a damned good thing. Ray Taylor was simply wishful thinking.

She crossed the room as the band put away their equipment.

Cole and Ray stood facing one another, deep in conversation, both apparently unaware of her presence. She glanced from one to the other.

Cole represented time-tested certainty. Ray was the deep blue sea, uncharted and unconquerable. She was too old to start testing the waters again. Wasn't she?

Leone walked toward the duo, stepped up to Cole and kissed his cheek.

When he turned to her the light that she expected to be there was missing. In its place was a look of resolve. A look that settles over someone who has wrestled long and hard with a decision.

The muscles of her stomach tightened as a flash of heat spread through her limbs.

She touched his shoulder, suddenly afraid and uncertain. Glancing briefly at Ray, she offered him a tight smile.

"Hello, fellas," she said, forcing a lightness into her voice. "You all were sounding really good."

"Ray and I were discussing some changes I'm making." His voice was flat, devoid of the warmth he usually reserved for her.

"Changes?" She looked anxiously from one to the other. Ray glanced away.

"I'll talk with you about it in the office," Cole said. "Okay, guys, that's it until later."

Rather than the usual exuberance the band displayed after rehearsal, they were extremely subdued, Leone noticed, a warning bell sounding in her head. But nothing could have prepared her for Cole's bombshell.

THIRTEEN

"What's going on?" Leone asked the instant the office door closed behind her. She put her purse on the desk and eyed Cole—waiting.

He kept his back to her. "I've been doing a lot of thinking, Lee, and I've decided it's time for some changes—around here and in my life."

Slowly he turned around and she felt her stomach flutter as if butterflies had been let loose.

"What kind of changes?" She stepped closer, her fingers worrying the bottom button of her blouse. The desk separated them, but it felt like a shaky bridge.

Cole straightened and inhaled deeply. All night he'd debated with himself about his decision, about what all this would mean, if he was doing the right thing. By sunrise he understood he had no other choice.

"I'm leaving the club, Leone."

The air stuck in her throat. The room suddenly grew warm, uncomfortable.

"What do you mean, leaving? I—don't—" She swallowed, tried to still the erratic pounding of her heart. "Why?" She came around to his side of the desk and placed her palm on his chest. "What is it, Cole? Talk to me. Are you ill?"

"No. I'm not sick. It's nothing like that," he said with that same emptiness that was terrifying her.

He turned away, moving toward the far side of the room. It was easier if he didn't have to look into her eyes.

"Cole." Her confusion escalated to panic. How would she manage without him? And with that question, she knew with certainty that it wasn't the club she was thinking about. The thought that he was leaving her terrified her. Terrified her the same way the dissolution of her marriage had terrified her. For all the years of her marriage she'd been brainwashed by Steven into believing that she was nothing without him. That she'd never make it if he was out of her life. She'd begun to believe it, accepted it as true. And when the divorce was final, he had glared at her in the courtroom, and said, "Wait and see. Before long you'll come back. You'll never make it on your own. All you know how to do is empty bedpans."

For months after, she was in a trance, moving through her days by rote. Expecting at any moment that the rug of life would be pulled out from under her. But it wasn't, and little by little she realized that she could stand on her own, could make a life without Steven. Yet, there was always that nagging doubt in the back of her mind, lying dormant, waiting for an opportunity to remind her how weak she really was.

That's how she felt right at that moment, weak and vulnerable. The rug of life was slipping from beneath her feet. And all she could do to keep from falling was retaliate.

"So out of the blue you tell me you're leaving. Just like that, with no thought to anything or anyone but yourself," she lashed out.

"It's time I started thinking about myself." He faced her. "I want to move on, move forward. I can't do that here. I can't do that with you."

The sting of his words held her paralyzed. There was so much she wanted to say. All the words were there, in her head, in her heart. But she couldn't get them out. All she could think of was that, again, in some way, she hadn't measured up. Couldn't cut it. A wave of nausea lifted her stomach.

"Cole..."

"We want two different things, Leone, you and I. I love you and...maybe you love me, too, in your own way. But I want more than just some time, Lee. I want more than just a few exhausted hours every now and then. And right now that's all you're willing to give." He drew in a breath. "And knowing how I feel and what I want, I can't stay on at the club—seeing you—it wouldn't work."

She reached out to him, and a sadness such as she'd never known filled her when he moved away, her fingers brushing air. "Please. Let's talk about this."

"What is there to say, Lee? If you can tell me I'm wrong, look me in the eye and tell me I'm wrong—I'll stay."

She started to say the words, wanted to say the words, just blurt them out, tell him he was wrong. But pride held her back. Once in her life she'd pleaded, begged, given in, just to be loved, have someone, and Steven had left her broken. She was still picking up the pieces.

"I—"

He held up his palm. "Don't, Lee," he said, his voice heavy with regret. There was that small corner, that one part of his soul that had hoped she'd tell him how wrong he was. "You don't have to make me feel better. It's cool." He looked away. "I'll finish out the rest of the month, give you a chance to find a replacement."

Suddenly she snapped out of her bout of self-recrimination, and retaliated with anger—an emotion she could handle. "A replacement? You seem to have this all figured out, some preconceived plan going according to your schedule. Things didn't happen in your time frame so you leave. Is that it?" she demanded, needing to attack him, turn the tide away from her and drown him in her pain.

"You know it's not that simple."

"Then why don't you explain it to me, since I'm too dumb to understand." Her eyes began to fill. Don't just walk out on me like Steven did, she thought. Not that.

"Lee, for you things are the way you've dreamed they'd be. The club is prosperous, your life is in order." He swallowed. "I've done all I can. It's time for me now."

Her head felt cloudy, her thoughts fuzzy, as if she were struggling with the after-effects of sleeping pills. She looked at Cole. Really looked at him and saw the unhappiness etched onto his rugged face. A heaviness that resided beneath his eyes from a lack of sleep, she was sure. But there was a purpose to his stance, a determination in the solid body she'd come to intimately know.

Her chest constricted painfully. She knew this man. She'd shared his secrets, her dreams, but she hadn't shared all of herself. She'd been too afraid. She knew that now. And that was all he'd ever asked for. The one thing she'd been unable to give and didn't know if she ever could. He deserved better.

She lowered her head, no longer able to bear the look of disappointment in his eyes.

"What will you do?" she managed to ask, but wanted to know what she would do without him.

He shrugged, picked up some papers on the desk as if they'd suddenly become important. "Travel a little, relax a lot." He offered a bittersweet smile. "Maybe I'll go visit my brother Calvin in San Francisco for awhile."

"Will—I see you? Talk to you?" She wouldn't cry.

"That's really up to you, Leone. Maybe when you figure out what you want."

"What makes you think that I haven't?"

"I'd say that was pretty obvious, wouldn't you?" He took his jacket off the hook. "I have some errands to run before the first set."

He moved past her toward the door. With one word she could stop him, convince him that this was all wrong. But she didn't.

The door closed quietly behind him.

FOURTEEN

"He said he'd finish out the month," Leone mumbled into her second cup of coffee for the morning.

Antoinette sat on the opposite side of Leone's kitchen table. "Out of the blue?" The absurdity of the situation raised her voice a notch. "That doesn't sound like the Cole I know."

Leone nodded in agreement, still unable to digest it all herself.

"What's happening with you? How do you feel about it? What did you tell him?"

Leone hesitated, ashamed almost of what she was about to say, but most of all confused by the way she had handled the whole thing.

"I'm not sure how I feel," she admitted. "On the one hand, I'm hurt and disappointed. On the other, I keep thinking that maybe it's for the best, that somehow I made it happen." She gazed into Antoinette's eyes searching for understanding.

"I'm with you on the first part, but I'm having some trouble with the second half. That sounds like some of the garbage Steven used to put in your head. Everything that went wrong, wasn't right or could have been better was your fault. How do you figure this is your fault?"

Leone took a long breath. "I guess I knew all along that I wasn't putting all my energies, my total heart, into our relationship. I took it for granted that Cole would always be around."

"Listen, girl, let's be honest. Steven put you through the wringer with his petty jealousies and constant campaign to undermine your self-esteem. He did everything he could to control your life, Lee. And whether you want to admit it or not, you haven't fully recovered from the effects."

Leone took a sip of her coffee. She knew Antoinette was right. Steven Weathers looked like a dream, and to the casual observer he acted like one. Everyone who'd ever seen the two of them together always commented on what a wonderful looking couple they made. No one really knew, except Antoinette, what went on behind their closed doors. And in the early days of their courtship and marriage, Leone was too blinded by love and awe to notice what was really happening to her. It was the little things, at first.

She remembered one date in particular. They'd been seeing each other for about six months and had been invited to a major fund raiser for the development company Steven worked for. She'd spent weeks shopping for the perfect dress and shoes. She'd had her nails done and hair cut into what she believed was an attractive style. She'd even spent half her morning getting a facial and new makeup. She wanted everything and herself to be perfect when Steven arrived.

Promptly at seven o'clock her doorbell rang. She was living in a studio at the time, and although it was beautifully furnished and perfect for one person, she longed to finish her RN training so that she could make some real money and get a bigger place. But maybe she wouldn't have to. If things kept moving along the way they had been between her and Steven, she might just become Mrs. Steven Weathers with a house of her own.

She took one last look in the mirror on her way to the door. Taking a breath, she pulled the door open, eager to see the look of pleasure on Steven's face when he saw her.

"Hi," she beamed, smiling with all the eagerness that raced around inside her.

Steven shot his pristine white cuffs and checked his watch. "We're going to be late if we don't leave right now. I thought I'd asked you to meet me downstairs." He glanced around, his smooth, pale brown features congealing in distaste as if he'd suddenly smelled something rotten. "You know how I hate to come through that lobby, not to mention that pissy, smelly elevator." He brushed off the sleeves of his midnight blue jacket, ridding it of imaginary lint.

Leone was a flower, wilting, withering under the scalding heat of his scorn that rained down upon her. One by one her beautiful petals fell to the earth, until there was nothing left but a thin bare stem ready to be cast aside.

"Come on, let's go. You know I hate walking into any place late."

It didn't occur to him that they couldn't leave until he had arrived, which he'd just done, Leone fumed, on the verge of tears. I have to walk through the same lobby and ride the same elevator, she thought, grabbing her purse and evening jacket.

For the entire evening while Steven charmed one guest after the other, Leone was left by herself, not introduced to anyone. And as the evening dragged mercilessly onward, the more insignificant she felt, shrinking by degrees into the floral patterns of the wall covering.

She should have left him then, but she didn't. She married him instead. Because Steven, being the charmer that he was, would always find ways to make it up to her. He'd take her home and make love to her as if she were the last woman in the world, the most incredible creature he'd even been with. He'd send flowers out of the blue, or surprise her by being parked outside of the hospital when she got off work. And she'd forget the hurts, the slights, the bouts of insecurity. Until she couldn't take it anymore. Couldn't take the arguments, the accusations, the ridicule.

"Why did you marry me, Steven?" she'd shouted. "If I'm such a disappointment to you, why did you marry me?"

He turned calmly toward her and delivered his parting line as calmly as a weather forecast. "You needed someone like me to take care of you, Leone. I felt sorry for you." He'd walked down the hall and shut the bedroom door.

In all her life she'd never felt so empty. She couldn't even feel hurt or anger, just nothingness. The following morning she found a lawyer in the Yellow Pages and filed for a divorce.

Antoinette was right. She hadn't gotten over the pain, the destruction. And because of it, she'd been afraid to truly love again. Now it was too late for her and Cole and it would be unfair of her to ask him to wait for her. Wait for her to heal.

"Don't cry, babe," Antoinette whispered, stroking Leone's head.

Surprised, Leone wiped her cheeks and found them damp with tears. She shut her eyes and sniffed. "What am I going to do, Nettie?"

"You're going to deal with it, day by day. You're going to get to know yourself, Lee, who you are and what you really want from life and a relationship. And if it's Cole that you really want, you'll make that decision when the time comes."

"Suppose he doesn't wait?" Leone asked, her voice coated in a child-like plea to make everything all right.

Antoinette knew what Leone wanted her to say. But she'd never lied to her friend, and she wouldn't start now.

"That's a chance you're going to have to take, Leone. Win or lose."

"I suppose." She took a deep breath. "You haven't heard the best part yet."

"What's that?"

"Ray is taking over the band until they find someone permanent."

"Oh, shit."

"My sentiments exactly."

"So what's going to happen with the band, brotha?" Parker asked as he wheeled his dove grey Mercedes CLK on to the Brooklyn Bridge on their way to Ray's house.

"Cole talked like he was hoping somebody was going to step up to the plate when he dropped the bomb, but nobody did."

Parker frowned. "Man, pleeze, what's the problem? That's every musician's dream to have their own band. Come on."

"Not these brothers. I guess it's because they all have families and regular day jobs to think about. Taking over a band, managing one, ain't easy. You know that."

"Yeah, yeah. You're right, I guess." He impatiently drummed his fingers along the steering wheel as they crept through the rush-hour traffic. Suddenly he snapped his head in Ray's direction.

"What about you, man? You sure don't keep a day job, and unless you've been holding back on the 411, you don't have a wife and kiddies to worry about."

Ray had wondered how long it was going to take Parker to leap onto that tidbit of information. He'd hoped to share his news over a couple of drinks. But the way the traffic was inching along, it would be time for him to start work before they got to the other side.

"He asked me to do it," Ray finally confessed.

"He asked you?" Parker couldn't believe it. "You mean he asked you after everyone turned it down, right?"

"No."

"What?"

"Actually, he asked me before he broke the news to everyone else."

"Get outta here. You've only been with them a couple of months. What gives? You're not that good," he added, emphasizing each word. Ray was wicked on sax, but Parker measured his accolades with a teaspoon.

"Thanks. And since that's the way you feel about it, I'll keep the details to myself."

"Aw, come one. That's not something you keep to yourself. This is big. Something you've been waiting for most of your life."

That much was certainly true. It had been a long-term dream to have his own band, something he could settle with, write music for and possibly record with, instead of the intermittent recording gigs he sat in on when needed. It was cool, but not solid, steady. That's what he was looking for in his life now. He realized it more each day.

"You gonna tell me or what?" Parker questioned, easing around a turtle-moving station wagon and just making the light across the Flatbush Avenue Extension exit.

"All right, all right. Don't beg. I got to the club early one night last week, wanted to run through some numbers, you know. When I arrived, Cole was already there, which wasn't really unusual. But he seemed like he was caught up in his own world. He was just sitting at the piano, staring at the keys, didn't even hear me the first time I spoke to him."

"Hey, man," Ray greeted while propping his sax case against the side of the stage. He peered at Cole's profile, wondering if he had just been ignored or if the brother really didn't hear him.

"Fleming. You all right, man?"

Cole blinked, and slowly turned his head in Ray's direction. "Hey, what's happening?" His voice was flat, dull like a floor that had been waxed one time too many. He aimed for a smile, but it missed its mark.

Ray stepped closer, slid his hands in his pants pockets. The club was only partially lit, casting shadows in some spots, plunging others into darkness. The view of Cole seated at the piano was obscured by the play of light that moved across his face. Yet Ray could still identify the mask of a troubled man.

Ray crossed the expanse of the stage. "Everything cool?" he asked while he pretended to look for some music sheets from the stand tucked away in the corner.

"Yeah. Yeah. Takin' it light. How about you?" Cole swung back toward the piano keys.

"You know how it is, still trying to get used to staying in one spot," he chuckled.

"I hear ya."

Cole cut his eyes in Ray's direction. "I know you must have a lady by now. You're real popular around here," he prodded.

"No one steady."

"Hmm. But I'm sure if the right opportunity presented itself…"

"Sure. If all the elements were right." The conversation was beginning to make him edgy. Did Cole sense his attraction to Leone? He'd tried to be cool, stay out of her way. But he got the impression that Cole was digging for something, but he couldn't figure out what.

"Let's say you had a steady gig, decent pay, great crib and the perfect lady, would you ever consider, hmm," he shrugged, "settling down, maybe heading up your own band?"

Ray's eyebrows met each other in the middle. Where was this going? Was he feeling him out to discover if he was planning to quit? He turned the question around in his head. Hey, the brother asked, so he must want to know the truth.

Ray pulled up a stool, slid it between his thighs and sat. He braced his palms on his knees and stared Cole directly in the eye.

"Fleming, as long as I can remember, having my own band was what I dreamed about. I've been all over the country, in and out of more dives than I could ever count. I've played with great bands and ones that should pack up their instruments and get day jobs."

They both laughed.

"I want to secure that dream. Yeah, I do," he said, his voice taking on the hush that fills you when real passion is the catalyst.

Thoughtfully, Cole nodded in agreement. He understood that gut feeling, that euphoria that lifts you, drives you until nothing else matters but the sound, the perfect note. He wanted to feel that way again, and because he didn't, he knew it was time to let it go.

"I was hoping that's what you'd say." Cole studied Ray a moment. Ray Taylor was on his way to greatness. He could see it, hear it, feel it. It was only a matter of time. "I want to make you an offer..."

"Just like that, huh?" Parker asked, finally making a left onto Atlantic Avenue. They passed one antique shop after another, the occasional restaurant, the YWCA on Third Avenue and then a string of Islamic bookstores and eateries. "So he offers you the deal of a lifetime, knowing that the other dudes won't take it?"

"Yep. He made his announcement, asked if anyone was willing to take over. When he got the negative response, he put my name up as his temporary replacement."

"Why you though?"

"'Cause I'm good at what I do," Ray tossed back.

"I suppose," Parker said with grudging admiration. "What did the rest of the band say?"

"They actually seemed relieved." He chuckled lightly.

"Man." Parker shook his head in disbelief.

Ray paused a beat. "We need a piano player."

The car jerked as Parker accidentally pressed too hard on the gas. "What are you saying?"

"I'm making my first executive request. You gonna help a brother out or what?"

Parker pursed his lips as if he was annoyed and totally put upon. "Thought you'd never ask."

Ray laughed.

"What about boss lady? What did she have to say?"

"Beats me. She hasn't been in for the past few days."

"Probably pissed and trying to regroup. Didn't you say the two of them had a thing going?"

"Yeah."

"Hey, maybe this is a bigger blessing in disguise than you thought it was."

"What's that supposed to mean?" He didn't want to think about what he just knew Parker was going to say.

Parker turned right on Flatlands Avenue, thought about detouring into the car wash, saw the line and changed his mind.

"It means, my brotha, the playing field is now open." He turned toward Ray and winked.

FIFTEEN

It was Sunday. The end of a long, tension-filled week. When Leone awoke she felt as if her body had been twisted into knots. Lying in bed, she stared up at the ceiling; the sounds of Raven's usual morning music was missing.

Friday evening she'd finally told Raven about Cole's leaving. She hadn't fully realized, or better yet, accepted how deeply Raven had become attached to Cole until she saw the pain on her face, heard it in her voice.

"Why?" Raven asked, her voice a whisper away from breaking. She wrapped her arms tightly around her thin frame as if she were trying to hold herself together. Her eyes filled and she blinked rapidly to stem the tears.

Leone lowered herself into a seat at the kitchen table, pressing her palms against the cool surface.

"He said he needed to make some changes in his life."

"I don't understand. He always seemed happy. He loves working at the club. He told me so." She dropped her arms defiantly to the side. "It's because of your relationship, isn't it?" she challenged. "He told me he wanted to marry you and make us a family."

"Things change, Raven. People change. That doesn't mean Cole stopped caring about us."

Raven stared at her mother for a long moment. "Where's he going?"

"He said he wants to go to San Francisco for a while to visit with his brother."

"Fine. Good riddance." She turned on her heel and stormed out of the room.

She probably could have handled the whole situation better, Leone thought. But the truth of the matter was, she didn't know what to say. For the most part, she was as confused as Raven. Although she was pretty certain her lack of being able to commit was part of the problem, she couldn't believe that was the only reason for Cole's abrupt announcement.

Leone turned onto her side. It had been nearly two weeks since he'd made his declaration. Although they were polite and pleasant to each other, the strain was unmistakable. And now that Ray was band leader and manager, they were thrown together more often than she would have liked. It certainly didn't make it easier on her with him turning up every minute. Sometimes she would be in the storeroom taking inventory and she'd feel his presence. She'd turn and he'd be standing there in the doorway, claiming that he needed to ask her a question. Or she'd be working in the office and he would pop up, earlier than the rest of the band for rehearsal, and sit with her until the guys arrived.

She hated it and anticipated it at the same time. When he wasn't around she would be disappointed, annoyed almost and let down. The whole thing was making her crazy. What did that say about her feelings for Cole? If she could feel herself heat from the inside out when Ray Taylor entered a room, was what she felt for Cole ever real? The more she thought about it, the less she knew.

She frowned. Cole had even gone so far as to tell her that she should be the one to teach Ray the business end of Soul to Soul, so that he would understand their system and help her out since he was leaving.

It was almost as if this were some divine plan of Cole's to put Ray solidly in her path. But why? She shook her head. That was just crazy thinking on her part.

Sighing, Leone peeped at the bedside clock. It was nearly noon and she had yet to rouse herself for the day. Tossing the light blanket aside, she pushed herself into a sitting position.

The new guy that was to take Cole's place on piano was supposed to sit in on a special rehearsal session later that afternoon, Leone recalled as she headed to the master bath for a shower. She was to be there as well to hear him play. She wasn't looking forward to it. It just made everything so final. In her mind no one could replace Cole.

She turned on the shower full blast. The more she thought about it, the more she realized that she was losing her enthusiasm for the club, for everything in general. She usually made it a point to visit the hair salon once a week, get her nails and toes manicured, and pick up at least one trinket for her and Raven in celebration of the end of the week. She hadn't done any of those things since Cole made his intentions known. Her bedroom, which she generally kept immaculate, showed signs of neglect. Clothes that should have gone to the cleaners had taken up residence across the chaise lounge. And she and Raven had eaten either pizza, Chinese food, or McDonald's for the past two weeks, since she didn't feel like preparing her usual full course dinners. Funny, Raven didn't seem to care or notice. It was if a general malaise had settled over both of them.

Leone pulled her soft green gown over her head and hung it on the back of the bathroom door. Little by little, day by day, she dreaded going to work. At first she thought it was because of the tension between her and Cole.

She stepped beneath the pulsing spray. But what she'd begun to understand was that much of her joy over the past year at the club had been because of Cole. His nurturing, attentiveness and love had been much of the driving force that kept her going. Falling in love with him had been an added bonus, yet one she had let slip away because of battles within herself.

Lathering her body with her favorite peach-scented soap, she realized with a deep sadness that settled like an anvil inside her stomach, that with Cole's leaving, her entire life was about to change.

Moments after Leone finished drying off, she heard the faint sound of the doorbell. Usually, the bell or the phone was Raven's cue to yell, "I got it!"

Leone listened. Nothing. Shaking her head, she quickly pulled a powder blue t-shirt over her head, zipped her jeans and slipped a pair of black leather mules on her feet. It was probably one of Raven's friends anyway.

Raven's withdrawal and anger were really worrying her. She'd had no idea that Raven would react so strongly, take it so personally. But she should have expected it. Raven's attachment to Cole over the past year was nothing short of phenomenal. His influence in her life had made her bloom, mature in a way. She was more focused on her schoolwork. Her choice of

friends had dramatically improved and her sense of
self as well as her blossoming womanhood were daily
becoming apparent. She'd become more open, actually happy. Not the strident, bitter girl who'd been
abandoned by her father at a time when she needed
him most. It wasn't so much the fact that her parents
were divorced. It was that Steven, in his inherent self-
ishness, had divorced himself from his daughter as
well. If he called once a month in the years since he'd
moved out, it was a lot. That alone had devastated
Raven in a way that Steven would never understand.
But somehow Cole did.

Leone headed downstairs. Maybe she should give
Cole a call and ask him to talk with Raven. Perhaps
coming from him, some assurance from him that he
still cared, that it wasn't her fault, she'd accept it better.

The bell rang once more, just as she entered the
foyer.

"Coming!"

As she approached she could just make out Cole's
form through the beveled glass window of the door.

For an instant, her breath seized in her chest, esca-
lating the beat of her heart. It was that old feeling, the
sensation she'd experienced when they first met. Too
late now, she cautioned herself. She took a breath,
straightened her shoulders and opened the first door.
Stepping into the vestibule, she put a smile of sorts on
her face and opened the outer door.

"Hi," she greeted, suddenly feeling awkward and
unsure. The light but manly scent of him, that familiar scent, filled the small space that separated them.
His cool, brown complexion was smooth, his hair
trimmed, his mustache neat, gently outlining the lips

that had touched her in the most intimate of places. Her pulse raced as she tried to beat back the rush of emotions that suddenly sprung to the surface, rekindling the smoldering embers that she had let die down. Too late, she cautioned herself. He's made his decision.

She kept her hand on the door frame, searching his rugged face for some clue as to why he'd come, then wondering if he still read her mind.

"I know I should have called. I was just cruising around and thought if you wanted—I could drive you to the club to listen to rehearsal," Cole said in that voice that could have easily been Barry White's equal. She'd often teased him about that, he recalled, and in return he'd croon some of her favorite Barry White hits and they'd roll all over the bed laughing in each other's arms. He swallowed as the knot of recollection welled in his throat. That wasn't why he was here— not to dredge up old memories. She had to want and need him as much as he wanted her. He needed to hear her say the words. But he wouldn't settle for anything less, not at this stage in his life.

"I—was going to call you," she said.

"Were you?"

His tone was skeptical, Leone noted, but she couldn't blame him. "Yes. About Raven, actually."

Cole's features tightened as if a string had been pulled beneath the skin. "What happened? Is something wrong?" He looked beyond her shoulder into the house as if the answer rested just beyond his line of vision.

Leone angled her head toward the interior. "Come in."

"She's completely shut down, and shut me out," Leone concluded as she sat opposite Cole at the island counter in the kitchen. "She's yet to come out of her room for the day."

"Dammit!" he suddenly exploded, slamming his palm on the surface. "I hadn't thought about how this might affect Raven. I figured she'd probably shrug it off like most teenagers do about things."

"I guess you didn't realize how important you are to her." She didn't mean to sound bitter and accusatory, but she couldn't help it. Being hurt was one thing. She was an adult and would deal with it. Raven, on the other hand, was still impressionable, still forming her values and ideals about men and relationships. And the only examples Raven had seen were failed ones. Her mother's.

Leone saw the pained look on Cole's face. She should apologize, she thought. But she didn't. She was hurting in a way she couldn't explain and she wanted him to hurt, too.

Cole averted his gaze. "Do you think she'll talk to me?"

Leone's right eyebrow rose in question. "Maybe. I can ask."

"Would you?"

She nodded in agreement and stood. She headed for the living room which led to the stairs. Just before she mounted them she stopped and turned back toward Cole.

"She loves you, you know," Leone said simply, needing him to understand the power that he held over her child.

"And I love her, too."

Leone pressed her lips into a tight smile and went in search of Raven.

Several moments later Raven appeared in the archway, body tense and expression sullen. Leone waited several feet behind her.

Cole stood, greeting her with a tender smile. "Hi, hon. How are you?" He wanted to hug her, take the look of sadness out of her eyes. But he dared not.

"Fine." She folded her arms and rested her weight on her right side.

"I thought you might want to go for a drive."

"For what?"

"Raven!" her mother snapped. "Don't be rude."

Cole held up his hand. "It's okay, Lee."

"Sorry," Raven mumbled.

He looked at Raven. "So, how 'bout it?"

Raven pouted for a moment, then glared at her mother. "All right. I need to change clothes."

"Take your time. And bring a jacket. It's pretty cool outside."

Raven trotted upstairs, leaving Cole and Leone by themselves.

Cole rose and began to pace the kitchen floor, needing to create some distance between him and Leone. Their close proximity was getting to him. The scent of her freshly scrubbed body was like an aphrodisiac. He wanted to take her in his arms, feel her weight against him. Would she let him if he tried? His spirit couldn't risk the rejection. Instead, he talked about mundane things.

"I can't believe how chilly it's gotten so quickly. Winter will be here before you know it."

Leone focused on his back that was turned to her. "You'll miss all that in California," she said.

Her words penetrated him like the plunge of a butcher's knife.

"Yeah, I suppose. Just have to deal with the occasional earthquake," he said, attempting to make his voice light.

"Hmm. Would you like something to drink?"

"Naw. I'm good." He turned. "So how have things been with you? We really haven't had a chance to talk lately."

"Fine. Busy," she responded, noncommittal. "And you?"

He shrugged. "Just trying to get everything together for this move." He chuckled. "You don't realize how much junk you accumulate until you get ready to relocate."

A tightness pulled in her chest. "You're taking everything?" she asked, suddenly realizing that this was no temporary jaunt to the coast.

"Whatever I can. What I can't, I guess I'll get rid of."

"So...this...isn't temporary? You intend to stay there."

Cole slid his hands into the pockets of his khaki slacks. "That's the plan, Leone. Make a clean break and start over."

She looked away. In her mind she'd always believed that it was just for a visit, short-term. That he'd come back and somehow they would work out whatever it was that had gone wrong. Give each other some time and space to listen to their hearts. She hadn't been willing to accept the idea that it would be for long, for good. She swallowed as an incredible ache gripped her insides, twisting them into a painful knot. Her eyes began to burn.

"I see." She exhaled and forced a smile. "I'm sure you'll love it out there. I hear it's wonderful."

"Yeah. I have some job offers lined up." He waited a beat. "Actually, I heard from one of them on Friday. It's a nightclub in Vallejo."

Her heart banged in her chest.

"They want me to come down next week. Rehearse with the band."

Her eyes widened. "Next week?"

He nodded. "That's the real reason why I stopped by, Lee. I, uh, I'll be leaving on Saturday."

Saturday. Too soon. Too soon. I'm not ready. She clenched her hands. "I see. Well," she breathed, "I'm, uh, glad everything is working out, that you're getting what you want." She rose and walked toward the cabinets, needing something immediate to do.

"Did you say you wanted some tea? I think I'll make some," she rambled, her thoughts and emotions in disarray.

All you have to say is don't go, Cole, and I won't, he thought as he watched her go through the motions of putting on the tea. Say it, Lee. Say it, he silently begged her. But she didn't.

"Sure you don't want some? I found this great cranberry blend." She felt as if she were coming apart, seam by seam as if someone had inadvertently pulled the single thread that held her together. Leave, why don't you? she wanted to scream. Just get out and go. Go to California. Run, don't walk. But she couldn't say anything.

"I'm ready," Raven announced, cutting through the tension that held the room and its occupants captive.

Cole stole a glance at Leone, hoping to see some sign, some inkling that there was still a chance. But she'd turned her back to him.

He took in a breath. "Then let's get going, kiddo." He crossed the room and put his arm around Raven's shoulders. "You hungry?"

"Always," she giggled.

"How 'bout some Mickey D's for starters?"

"Super size," she warned, gazing up at him.

Cole glanced over his shoulder. "See you later. At rehearsal."

All Leone could do was nod her head.

SIXTEEN

Leone didn't wait for Cole to return. She couldn't take the chance that if she was alone with him, she'd beg him to change his mind; humiliate herself by pleading for his love; use her body to make him stay; whisper promises so that he wouldn't go.

So instead she got in her car and drove. She had no destination in mind and drove by rote, barely noticing the stroll of lovers, mothers with children in tow, hurrying home from church to fix Sunday dinner, the determined joggers, or the outlandish clothes and hairstyles of the teens who traveled in bands of three to ten.

In the middle of all things familiar, she felt lost, disconnected, as if someone had spilled coffee on the roadmap of her life, smearing all the landmarks. The street in front of her became cloudy, and she realized that she was crying, silently weeping for what was and what might never have the chance to be.

Reaching the mouth of downtown Brooklyn, Leone took the exit onto the Brooklyn Queens Expressway, better known as the BQE to traffic-weary New Yorkers. The spanning highway wrapped around the boroughs, linking the multi-ethnic hub of Queens to the plethora of cultural expansion in Brooklyn. However, in the back of her mind good sense prevailed and she quickly remembered how easy it was to get lost on the streets of Queens. It seemed that each little community had a secret society dedicated to confusing drivers and pedestrians with a multitude of similarly numbered streets, roads, places and lanes. She took the next exit, which put her onto the Belt Parkway East.

As she sped along the familiar roadway, she drove abreast of the shoreline. On the horizon she could see the water dotted with the colorful sails of small crafts, the boardwalks lined with would-be fisherman—even though the fish were not fit to eat, fishing was still a pleasant pastime. She passed the riding stables and caught a glimpse of equestrians in training. Much farther ahead she saw the peaks of the towering buildings that comprised Starrett City, the complex built on what was once the swamplands of Brooklyn. Winding her way around, she spotted in the distance the houses that ran along the waterfront. The scene brought to mind a sleepy village and she wondered what it really looked like close up. Seeing an exit coming up, she veered right and got off, now with a destination in mind.

Somehow she found her way into the Flatlands, each street number in consecutive order with winding cul-de-sacs and dead ends hidden by towering trees which hung like green canopies across the roads and the exquisite homes.

It was a part of the city she'd never ventured into before and she roamed aimlessly, taking in the beauty until she realized she'd pulled into a neat cluster of four homes that were braced by the water. She pulled to the end of the drive and was in the middle of making a U-turn to get out when she spotted someone coming out of the house to her right.

For an instant her heart stopped, then began a rapid beating. Ray.

This was a private community, which was one of the reasons Ray had finally decided to settle down there. He never had to concern himself with the blare of police sirens, loud music and bands of high-strung teens. Yet with all the privacy the area afforded, he was less than five minutes away from the rest of the world. The owners of the four houses that sat in the circular cocoon all knew each other and looked out for trespassers. So the sight of an unfamiliar vehicle, with its engine running, immediately caught his attention.

He stood on the edge of his property and tried to get a closer look without being too obvious. After all, whoever it was could be a visitor for one of his neighbors. He dropped his bag of garbage into the can but didn't take his eyes off the car which was beginning to look familiar. He squinted, hoping to get a better view of the occupant, because he was certain it couldn't be who he thought.

Oh, Lord, Leone thought. How in the world am I going to explain this? I know he must recognize me by now. He probably thinks I'm staking out his house or something. She turned the car around with the intention of speeding off as if she didn't see him, when he suddenly smiled and waved.

Briefly she shut her eyes. When she opened them he was coming toward her, with that swagger straight out of a shoot 'em up Western. As he drew closer, she could see the light of surprise sparkling in his eyes. He leaned down and she reluctantly lowered the window.

He grinned broadly, truly surprised at seeing her. "What are you doing around here? Visiting?" He braced his forearm on the doorframe, his face inches away from hers.

"Uh, no. Actually I was just driving around. I, uh, spotted the area from the highway. I'd never been around here before..."

"Well, come on out. I'll give you a tour."

She shook her head as she spoke. "No, really, I..."

"Come on." He angled his head to the side. "Personal tour? Can't beat that."

She mulled it over a minute. What harm could it do... really? After all, she was there already. "All right. Where can I park?"

"Just pull up behind my car in the driveway right there." He pointed toward his house and stepped back so she could pull her car around.

At least she looked halfway decent, she thought, cutting the engine. Well almost, except for the fact that her eyes were probably red and swollen from crying. She took a quick peek in the mirror and cringed. She could always blame it on allergies.

Taking her bag from the passenger seat, she opened the door and got out.

Ray took her in with one long glance. He wished he understood what it was about Leone that had him walking on eggshells. Around her he felt inept, inexperienced, as if he somehow had to try to prove his worth to her. A part of him believed that she saw him as a talented but unambitious skirt chaser with nothing more on his mind than a good time. He didn't know why what she thought of him was important, but it was. That Sunday afternoon that they'd spent in the club together had definitely broken the ice, but even after that she still remained reserved and aloof. Almost as if their whole conversation, the trip home and what almost happened, never transpired.

Maybe it was best, he thought, watching her long legs bring her closer to him. After all, regardless of the circumstances, she was still Cole Fleming's woman. And until somebody told him otherwise, he would make every attempt to act accordingly. However, he really had to question the fates for having dropped her virtually in his lap. What was that supposed to mean?

Leone's legs felt like strings of cooked spaghetti, and she wondered if she looked as wobbly as she felt. She plastered a smile on her face.

"You really don't have to do this, you know," she said immediately.

"Of course I don't. But I'd like to. Come on inside."

Ray stepped ahead of her and she took a deep breath and followed him in.

When she crossed the threshold, she would have sworn she'd stepped into the virtual world of Architectural Digest or House Beautiful. Wood and glass dominated the two-story structure, beginning with a sunken living room that boasted rafters and track lighting, and a wrought iron, spiral staircase. The open-air living room gave a clear view of the dining room, the kitchen, and the water beyond. And if she wasn't mistaken, there was a small boat docked right behind his house. Built-in smoke glass units contained cut crystal and china on one wall and CDs, cassettes, a massive stereo system, and bar on the other.

The deep carpet was such a pale beige it was almost white, which was in sharp contrast to the deep forest green leather furniture that dotted the space. Art was strategically placed along the winter white walls leading to the floor above and surrounding the living space.

"Wow," was all she could finally mutter. Her gaze continued to wander around the room.

Ray chuckled. "That seems to be the first response from everyone who comes here. You get used to it after a while." He headed for the bar and opened the glass door. "It's comfortable, fills my need for the ultimate in style...and it's private." He took out a bottle of Scotch. "Can I fix you a drink?"

"No. Nothing for me, thanks." She stepped down and moved toward the couch.

"Sure? Soda, water?"

"Hmm. Well, maybe a Coke if you have it."

"Comin' up."

"Great art," she commented, twisting her hands in her lap while noticing Basquiat, Catlett, Biggers and some Cynthia St. James originals. Impressive.

"Yeah, I try to collect things in my travels." He poured a glass of Coke, then turned on a John Coltrane CD. "Ice?"

"Yes. Thanks." She began to clutch her purse as if she could squeeze out the tension that ran through her like electric charges.

Ray handed her the glass of Coke and joined her on the couch. "You want to talk about it?" he asked softly. "I'm a pretty good listener."

"Talk about what?"

"Whatever drove you out of your house on a Sunday afternoon for starters." He took a sip of his drink.

"Maybe I like driving around."

"True. I know with me, when I get in the car with no specific destination in mind it's usually because I need to clear my head. Driving does that for me. What about you?"

Leone stared into her glass, watching the ice cubes swim around in the brown, bubbly liquid. "I suppose," she mumbled.

"Did it help?"

"What?"

"The drive."

Leone shrugged. "Not really," she admitted. She released a breath. "I guess it's too complicated."

"Sometimes talking helps. But if you'd rather not, I understand." He leaned back against the cushions of the couch.

"I thought you were bringing in the new piano player today."

"I am." He checked his watch. "We're supposed to meet at the club at six. I still have a few hours."

"Oh."

They were both quiet for a moment, the strains of Coltrane's sax wafting in the background with his rendition of "My One and Only Love."

"We never really had a chance to talk again...since that Sunday afternoon...in my car."

Leone swallowed.

Ray eased a bit closer. He knew what he was about to do was wrong, but he didn't want to think about it because if he did...

He took her chin between his fingers and turned her to face him. "I wanted to kiss you then, Lee." He searched her eyes, let his gaze trail down her face to her throat and saw the tiny pulse beat there. "I want to kiss you now. I want to know what it feels like."

She should stop him, just get up and leave. Her car was right outside. But she could no more stop his lips from meeting hers than she could stop the racing of her heart.

They were soft, moist, experienced as his mouth played with hers, gently urging her to open her lips, let him explore her depths. And by degrees she did.

Their tongues met in an explosive dance that shot straight to her head. White light blinded her and she ceased to breathe as she swallowed the deep moan that he exhaled. It settled inside her, gentle at first then building like a volcano ready to erupt, building, building.

His fingers, long and sinewy, trailed along the sides of her face, across her shoulders, then down her arms until he gathered her against him.

She twisted her body to get closer, closer as the heat between them intensified like flames fanned by a roaring wind. The exquisite power of it made her lose all sense of reason and all she knew for certain was that she wanted more. She wanted to feel his hands on her body, on her bare flesh. She wanted to touch him.

Tentatively her fingers played with the buttons of his denim shirt. Ray clasped her hand and held it against his heart. She took his other and placed it against hers.

"Lee," he whispered against her mouth. "Tell me it's okay," he uttered in a voice so deep it was hardly recognizable.

"Yes," came her ragged reply.

His fingers splayed, covering her right breast, and she gasped as a tremor shot through her.

Little by little he increased the pressure until his touch became an ever-escalating torture. He eased back and looked into her eyes as he lifted her T-shirt over her head before freeing her breasts of the confines of satin and lace. He tossed her shirt and bra onto the floor.

For several moments he simply stared at her, transfixed by her soft beauty. Like one in awe, he touched the twin swells and she shuddered, her eyes slamming shut when his mouth covered the nipples that had hardened into dark fruits.

His mouth was hot as it took her in, his tongue laving the sensitive peaks until she whimpered with hunger. Cautiously he eased her back until his body covered hers. She immediately felt the hard knot of desire throb between her thighs that had grown wet with need and anticipation.

Slowly he moved against her, pressing his flesh into her, offering a mere sample of what it would feel like buried within her.

She was literally on fire. Every nerve ending pulsed as if electrified. And then his mouth, his tongue danced along her stomach, dipped into her navel even as he unfastened the button and zipper of her jeans, easing them down her thighs.

All that separated him from her was a thin band of baby blue fabric. Tenderly he touched her there and her body tensed.

"It's okay," he soothed, stroking her as he placed tiny kisses all along the dark triangle that shadowed the near sheer fabric.

Her inner thighs quivered. And then suddenly she was alone. Her eyes flew open and Ray stood above her, staring down at her with a dark, brooding longing that was almost frightening in its power.

He unbuttoned his shirt and threw it to the floor, pulled his wallet from his back pocket and removed a sealed condom before stepping out of his pants and boxers.

He was beautiful, she thought, dizzily watching him cover his throbbing erection with the latex sheath. His body was a study of rippling muscle covered in a smooth brown satin. His thighs bulged like those of a runner, his stomach flat and firm, and for a brief moment she thought of her own. Nothing like it once was. Nothing like what she was certain he was accustomed to. And she knew her breasts no longer had the firm fullness of her youth. And suddenly she felt old. Old compared to this man who was ten years her junior.

"You're absolutely exquisite, Leone," he whispered, pushing aside her doubts. "More beautiful than I could have imagined." He lowered himself above her. "I'll make you happy." He separated her thighs with his own, bracing his weight on his arms.

Instinctively, she raised her knees, tightening them against his waist.

"I promise," he said before his tongue delved into her mouth and he eased deep into her warmth in one smooth stroke.

Her hips arched high against him, taking him in farther...more...letting him reach the deepest recesses of her body, filling her until there was nowhere to go...but in and out...try it again, over and over.

Ray kissed her mouth, her neck, suckled her breasts, whispered how good she felt in her ear, moved in a slow but steady rhythm into her body, marking his place time and again until she thought she would go mad if release didn't come.

He held her, it seemed, at the precipice where she was able to look into the lush valley of fulfillment, but he wouldn't let her take the plunge...not yet. He wanted her to remember this time between them, burn it into her body and her mind, as he knew it would be indelibly seared into his.

The feel of her beneath him, around him, had his mind swimming, his emotions raw. He'd been with many women in his life. All kinds of women. But not like this. Not like Leone. And the strength of it scared him. Scared him because he'd allowed his emotions to overrule his mind. He'd broken an oath that he'd promised himself he'd never break—sleep with another man's woman. Yet, knowing that, he couldn't help himself. Didn't want to. Consequences be damned. He'd waited all his adult life to feel like this with a woman...complete.

She rocked her hips against him and he sank deeper as the strangled cry of his name spilled from her lips.

He buried his face in her neck to keep from sobbing as the waves of an unspeakable climax surged through him, hardening him even further until it was only seconds before release shot through him, and the rhythmic pulse of her own orgasm sucked out the last of his life-giving fluids.

He collapsed against her and they held each other in a satiated silence. Their bodies shuddering with the aftereffects of their lovemaking. He looked into her eyes and saw tears glistening on her lashes. Gently he kissed them away.

Leone felt his weight, the wetness between her thighs, the throb that continued to pulse there, the tingle that still held her nipples taut and sensitive to the touch. Still their bodies moved against one another in tiny after-thrusts, seemingly unable to douse the

fire. And in the midst of the wonder of it all, her mind
screamed: What have I done?

The heat of his breath purred against her throat
while he steadily caressed her hip in a slow circular
motion. Involuntarily her insides gripped him and felt
him swell until his arousal peaked, filling her.

He groaned in sublime agony as wonton desire
seized him. She lifted her pelvis rocking against him.

Ray raised his weight onto his arms and gazed into
her eyes while he moved in an erotic dance. "It's all
right," he whispered, sensing her doubts, her struggle
with guilt. Gently he kissed her, gathered her tightly
into his arms, sealing their bodies, their souls together. "I promise you."

But how could it be? Leone wondered, even as the
electric waves of sensation spread through her limbs.
Yet, feeling Ray, being with him, sharing herself in
this way, seemed all too right, to be wrong.

"I didn't plan for this to happen," Ray said as they
sat next to each other on the couch. He twirled a
strand of her hair around his finger.

"But I'm glad that it did," Leone said, tucking his
shirt around her body, suddenly feeling naked. She
glanced across at him. "And I wasn't stalking you,"
she said with a hint of nervous laughter.

"Now I'm disappointed," he quipped. He waited a
beat. "So, what are we going to do now? What are you
going to do?"

Leone flinched. She didn't want to think about
that part. For as long as she could, she wanted to hold
onto the fantasy with Ray. And that's all that it was,
a fantasy. They were both adults. Something between
them had clicked and they'd connected. That didn't

mean they had to be life partners. They could both walk away, back to their lives and leave these past few hours behind. Couldn't they?

Leone cleared her throat, and tried to sound very 90s, like the women she was sure he was used to. "Really, it's no big deal. What happened, happened." She shrugged. "I mean, this isn't the first time for either of us," she continued with bravado. "And I'm sure it won't be the last—with other people," she qualified. "I say we move on. Take today as a great memory and move on." She pulled the shirt a bit tighter.

Ray stood, totally unconscious of his nude body, or the effect it had on her.

"Cool" was all he said. He crossed the room to the stairs. "I'm gonna take a shower, get some of this sweat off," he said in a way that suddenly made Leone feel dirty. "There's a guest bath just behind the kitchen if you want to do the same thing." He shrugged and smiled bitterly. "But, hey, maybe you don't."

He trotted up the stairs and didn't look back.

For several moments Leone simply sat there, unable to move. She'd never felt so cheap and ashamed in her life. Even at her lowest moments with Steven, she'd never felt so totally dehumanized.

She heard the sound of the shower beating against the walls, and her current situation became clear.

With determination, she gathered her clothing, took a shower, got dressed and into her car. When she pulled out of Ray's driveway, she had no intention of ever revisiting this day again.

Ray watched her pull away from between the slat of his bedroom blinds. Didn't she feel anything? he wondered. Couldn't she tell that with her it wasn't some casual fling? He expected that kind of response from some of the other women he'd been with, but not from her.

He turned away from the window and began to get dressed. He shouldn't be hurt, he thought, pulling on a black T-shirt. But he was. For the first time in his life he'd wanted to be more to a woman than a great lay. He wanted her to care, really care—about him.

Most of the time it didn't matter. He zipped his black jeans. But this time it had. He stepped into his black leather loafers.

But, he concluded, looking into the mirror and running a brush across his hair, if she can dismiss what happened between them as nothing more than a fling, then so could he.

The last place Leone wanted to go was to the club. She didn't think she could look Cole in the face knowing what had transpired between her and Ray.

And what of Ray? How could she face him as well? What must he think of her? It was obvious by his attitude afterward that he thought very little.

"Oh, God!" She slammed her palm against the steering wheel, inadvertently sounding the horn, much to the annoyance of the driver in the car ahead of her. When had she turned into the kind of woman who let her hormones make her decisions?

She took a shaky breath. Well, as the saying goes, she sniffed, you made your bed, now lie in it. "Or couch," she mumbled sarcastically as a tear of regret ran down her cheek.

Stopping for a red light, she reached for her cell phone and hit the programmed code for her house.

After the third ring, Raven picked up, sounding rushed and breathless.

"Hi, hon, it's me. How was your afternoon with Cole?" Her heart thumped.

"Fine. I just got back and heard the phone."

"Oh...uh...is Cole with you?"

"No. He dropped me off. Said there was a rehearsal with the new piano player."

Leone flinched. "Right. I'm on my way over there now."

Silence.

"Cole said I could come and visit him in San Francisco anytime I want and he'd pay for my ticket," Raven quickly added, assuring that money would never be a reason for her not to go.

"That's really nice of him."

"He said maybe I could convince you to come sometime, too."

Her throat tightened. The light turned green.

"Uh, I'll talk to you when I get home."

"Sure." Raven hesitated, then rushed the words out. "I don't know what happened with you and Cole, Ma, but whatever it is, you can still fix it. He really loves you."

Leone knew if she stayed on the line a minute longer, she'd burst into tears. Whatever repairs could have been made, it was too late now. Even though she and Cole weren't officially together, there was still that unspoken tenet that the possibility remained, and a tenuous thread still holding them together. If anything could have broken that thread, what happened today was it.

"I've really got to go, Raven. You know how nervous talking on this thing while I'm driving makes me.

I'll see you later. Okay?" She pressed the "end" button and slipped the phone back into its slot.

Leone moved along with the traffic and headed toward the club and uncertainty.

SEVENTEEN

"You did what?" Parker asked while he put on his jacket.

Ray paced back and forth across the wooden floor. "I slept with her," he repeated.

Parker shook his head in disbelief. "Hey, man, when I said the field was open, I didn't think you'd take me up on it." He picked up his knapsack from the corner by the couch and slid the straps over his shoulders. "So now what?" He opened the door.

Ray followed him outside. "I guess it's like she told me, we just move on."

"That's cool with you, man?"

Ray shrugged. "Sure, why not?"

Parker looked over his shoulder. Ray might be a lot of things, Parker thought, but a good liar wasn't one of them. "You like her a lot. And I don't think you're taking it as light as you want me to believe."

"Hey, it was what it was. No biggie." He shut the door behind himself.

"If you say so, man. But I don't believe you." Parker walked toward his car and opened the door. "My question is, how are you going to be able to look Cole in the face with her in the same room?" He gave Ray an arched look and slid behind the wheel of his Mercedes.

Ray got into his own car and started the engine. How was he going to face Cole? How could he hide his true feelings for Leone, especially now? He pulled out behind Parker and into traffic.

An anvil of guilt slammed down in his chest. Cole didn't deserve this. Not like this, even if everything wasn't perfect between him and Leone. He had no right to muddy the waters. Leone was vulnerable and at a shaky point in her life. And as much as he wanted her, making love with her wasn't the answer to what brought her to his door. He knew that, and yet, he'd let emotion instead of reason take over. He felt as if he'd taken advantage of her. Her need for him was not borne of genuine caring, but rather insecurity and the desire to be cared about, have her issues soothed by touch. She'd needed to feel wanted and worthwhile. At least, maybe, he'd been able to do that much. But at what cost?

Getting involved with another man's woman, be it a tenuous relationship or not, was something he'd never done. And, now, without question, he knew why.

Leone pulled onto the block of Soul to Soul, drove by looking from one side of the street to the other. She didn't spot Ray's car. She felt a momentary reprieve. Maybe he wouldn't show up, she thought in a silent prayer. But just as quickly, she knew that was an impossibility. Ray would show up. It wouldn't be like him not to, no matter what the circumstances.

She found a parking space around the corner from the club. For several minutes she sat in the car trying to get her thoughts and emotions in order. She took a quick peek in the mirror and dabbed at her eyes.

Maybe she should just go home. Put this off until she could think clearly.

"No," she said aloud. "Twenty-four hours or twenty-four days isn't going to change a thing."

She sucked in a deep breath. What happened between her and Ray was a done deal. They were two adults, she counseled herself. She and Cole hadn't slept together in nearly two months. They both knew that things had shifted between them but neither had been willing to let go. Maybe they didn't want to. In her heart she knew she didn't, but Cole had made up his mind and she didn't believe it was her right to change it, especially when her own emotional focus and level of commitment was so uncertain.

Taking her purse from the passenger seat, she opened the door, shut it behind her and walked toward the club.

You can do this, she repeated over and again in a silent mantra.

She took the keys from her purse and opened the club door. "You can do this," she whispered to herself one last time, and stepped inside.

Cole was seated on a stool on the stage chatting with the guys in the band. He turned in her direction when he heard the door.

The instant he saw her, he felt that old familiar heat warm his insides. God, he loved her and always would. Leaving her was the hardest thing he'd ever had to do. But he knew he must for his own emotional salvation.

Maybe with some time and space she would realize that they were meant to be together. But he knew he couldn't hang around. He couldn't stand knowing and seeing the looks that passed between her and Ray

Taylor, or live with the thought that Ray might touch her the same way he had, only better.

Maybe if he moved out of the way, gave them some space, she'd see that Ray Taylor could never give her half of what he could.

Ray was still young and ambitious. Still full of himself and his own dreams. He didn't honestly believe that Ray was truly ready for a serious commitment to anyone other than himself, no matter what he'd told him before.

Yet, he could be all wrong about Ray. He might be the man for Leone. It was risky, what he was doing. But it was a risk he was willing to take because he loved her. And above all else, he wanted Leone to be happy, even if her happiness was with someone else. At least he would know he'd tried.

Leone put on her best smile and hoped that in the dimness of the club, no one would see the tremulous edges.

She walked confidently toward the group.

"Hey, fellas."

There was deep chorus of hellos.

She put her purse down on a nearby table. "Just getting started?"

Cole stood. "We're just waiting on Ray and the new guy." He hopped down and stood in front of her. As soon as he did, he felt the change in her, the shift in the heat that her body gave off, the eyes that wouldn't quite meet his, and his heart stood still. Slowly his eyes glided over her but not in that tender way he usually reserved for her.

Could he see through her pretense? she wondered as her heart hammered in her chest.

"How are you?" he asked. "When I brought Raven home you were gone."

Her gaze darted away, roaming the room. She cleared her throat of the lie that sat there. "I just went for a drive. Ran some errands."

Cole stared at her a moment. "Oh, Raven was worried."

She turned back to him. "I called her." She paused. "Raven said you two had a good time."

"We did. And a good talk." He wanted to touch her as he used to, somehow uncoil the rope of tension that had wrapped around her body. "I think she understands."

"Does she?" she asked caustically. She could feel her anger and frustration rise to the surface. At least those were emotions she could handle.

"Don't do this, Lee," he cautioned, lowering his voice.

Her eyes snapped up and locked on his face. For an instant her heart softened and all she wanted to do was let him take her in his arms and make things between them the way they were. But she couldn't and neither could he.

"Do what? Be real?"

"No. Make this harder than it already is."

"For who, Cole? You or me?" She spun away, leaving him standing there, and retreated into the back office.

She shut the door firmly behind her and leaned with her back against it. Steeling herself she walked across the room and sat down behind the desk. She covered her face with her hands and cried.

∞

"This is it," Ray said as he and Parker approached the door to the club. "Just be cool," he warned, tapping on the glass.

"Don't know any other way to be, brotha. You be cool."

Ray glanced over his shoulder at Parker and sneered instead of smiled.

Earl, the band's drummer, opened the door. "Hey, man," he greeted, giving Ray a pound.

"Earl, this is my man, Parker."

The two men shook hands. "Good to meetcha. Come on in. We've been waiting on you guys."

Once inside, Ray made all the introductions and the band took their places. Behind them, near a corner of the stage, Al unzipped the protective case on his upright bass. The lanky chocolate man whistled the melody of "Autumn in New York" as he set up behind the others.

"I was thinking we'd do an all 'Bird' tribute tomorrow night," Cole suggested. "Some of the old bop standards."

Ray busied himself with adjusting the thick Rico reed on his shiny Selwen sax, not looking at anyone. The avoidance of eye contact was not lost on Cole, who pulled a fistful of charts from his leather tote.

"What tunes did you have in mind, Mr. Ivorys?" Al quipped, feeling the uneasy tension between the pair.

"Maybe 'Confirmation,' 'Ornithology,' 'Funky Blues,' or 'Au Privare,'" Cole said, a curious expression of bewilderment on his face.

"That's cool," Mel, the trumpeter, chimed in. He was always late and usually blessed out on Scotch, but his playing on brass easily matched the pyrotechnics of Dizzy, Fats, Little Jazzy or Miles.

"What do you think, Ray?" Cole asked, staring the young saxophonist in the face.

A silence followed, which only heightened Cole's certainty that something was wrong. Ray's eyes held an odd, faraway look, as if he was recalling a memory of joy in his head.

"Ray...Ray...Ray. Earth to Ray," Cole teased. "What's up, man? You're off on another planet. What do you think about the 'Bird' idea?"

Parker watched from the distance, ready to intercede if necessary. His boy was not putting on a good show.

"Yeah, I'm down with it," Ray answered absently, now staring in the direction of Leone who'd reentered the room.

The look, the distracted reply, the returned expression on Leone's face, made Cole even more uneasy. Something had happened between the two of them. He felt it. Thoughts flooded into his mind, sinister thoughts, forbidden thoughts, painful thoughts.

EIGHTEEN

Cole's gaze shifted from Ray to Leone, who'd both moved like shadows to opposite ends of the rehearsal space, as if by distance they could snap the band of tension in half.

Parker stepped forward, a human shield between Cole and Ray. "You want me to sit this one out, Cole?"

Cole blinked, and slowly focused on Parker.

"Naw, lemme hear what you can do."

Cole stepped down off the stage, but instead of taking a seat at the table with Leone, he sat two tables away. He leaned back in the chair, resting it on its hind legs.

"Ray, it's your show, man." He cut a look at Leone. "Go for it."

Ray moved to center stage. He placed the horn to his pursed lips, checking the reed and his embouchure. The room quieted suddenly. This was not big band Ray or even small group Ray; this was Ray alone. Solo.

His eyes closed and his entire body seemed to shudder before he launched into the soft, lyrical Ellington ballad, "Satin Doll."

Mel nodded in unison to the cute little phrases, the agonizingly beautiful lines full of a variety of feeling and mood.

Parker leaned back on the piano and smiled, taking in every improvised note and shift.

The music stroked Leone's battered soul, gentle, tentative like the brush of a feather along a sensitive spine. So sweet, yet a cry of exquisite torment, a need unrequited in each note, tumbling over her like pebbles skipping over water.

She was swept away, captured and helpless. Yet she didn't want to be released. It was as if Ray was speaking to her, pouring out his heart, emptying his soul. But he couldn't be. She wouldn't let him. But she felt him as surely as if his hands were on her bare flesh, scorching her, igniting every nerve.

Rocking slightly to the melody, Ray seemed to be deconstructing the song, adding in a host of new twists and turns. But as soon as the group grew accustomed to this gentle music that broke the rules, coming from somewhere deep in his soul, he cut loose, turning his sound into something hard, harsh and terrible. A roar that held a fierceness, a boldness that no one had ever heard in his playing before, not even Parker. Sounds that were a mix between Coltrane and Ayler.

Leone shut her eyes and trembled.

Mel stared into the bell of his trumpet, almost as if he was ashamed to witness this raw, naked part of Ray's inner terrain. No one said anything.

A long rush of caresses followed—something that spoke of confusion, frustration and pain. Ray bent over like a boxer who'd been sucker punched, reaching for more squawks and shrieks that made the hair stand on Leone's long, lovely neck. She sat there with tears in her eyes, glistening in the amber glow of the stage lights.

Cole rocked back in his chair, transfixed by what he was hearing. He never knew Ray had such deep feelings in his soul, never knew the young man could be so revealing, so honest. He also knew that this was not just magic, but a confession of love, of guilt, of betrayal.

Ray returned with his soft, molasses voice, the bass-throated tone that made the women sigh, before firing off a series of blues-colored notes in a long cluster, before howling like a man possessed, before finally ending in a raw sexual cry.

Cole observed Leone's expression shift from rapture to despair. She sat staring, mesmerized, as tears flowed down her cheeks. Suddenly, she heaved a sigh and hurried from the room.

Cole watched her leave, then turned back to face Ray on the stage. The young saxophonist abruptly stopped playing, holding the horn, Coltrane style, across his chest. For a moment, he locked glances with Cole, and once seeing the recognition of his sin in Cole's eyes, pivoted and walked off the bandstand. He didn't stop walking until he left the club.

No words were needed then. The truth had been told.

The room was suffused in a winter silence. The kind of quiet that settles in the morning hours after a long night of snow—serene—almost painful in its chilling beauty.

Cole slowly rose, shedding the cold cloak of his new reality.

"Guess it took Ray someplace else," he said quietly, not looking at anyone in particular. He tugged on his bottom lip with his teeth. "Heavy piece of work."

"I'll go get him," Parker announced.

"No. I'll go. Why don't you run through the next number. See what you can do with it, Parker."

All eyes followed Cole as he stepped outside.

When Cole came through the door, Ray was leaning against his car, arms folded, head bowed.

"Nice piece of work you did in there," Cole said, appearing in front of him.

Ray's head rose slowly, his gazed latched onto Cole's countenance, but wouldn't meet his eyes. He didn't respond.

"It takes a helluva man to do something like that— reveal yourself." A flicker of a smile appeared then vanished.

Ray looked away. "Yeah," was all he uttered.

Cole pulled out a pack of Newports from his shirt pocket. He lit a cigarette, and blew a cloud of smoke over Ray's head. "People say the eyes are the windows to the soul. I think music is the window," he said, his words trailing the white vapors. "When we open ourselves to it, it admits everything. Too much sometimes. Even the things we try to hide. Not everyone can understand the words being said through the notes...except maybe another musician."

Ray met his eyes for the first time and in them stood understanding. Perhaps not forgiveness, but acceptance.

Cole stamped out his cigarette, grinding it into crumbs on the gray concrete, turned and reentered the club, leaving Ray with his thoughts and his conscience.

NINETEEN

It had been nearly three weeks since that fateful afternoon at the club, and two since Cole had said his good-byes. He'd refused to allow Leone to accompany him to the airport, saying that it was best. The last time she saw him, he was packing up his music sheets and having a final drink with the gang.

Leone sat on the edge of her bed, lost in the storm that her life had become. She felt adrift, as if her anchor had been removed and she'd been cast out to sea with no destination.

What had she done? she asked herself for the umpteenth time as she walked toward the window. She pushed the pale green, gossamer curtains aside and stood framed in the window.

A light rain fell—mist really—casting a pall across the city. Ghost-like canopies hung above the homes, creating an image of the surreal.

The tip of her finger drew circles in the hazy moisture on the window, aimless circles until the glass was clear. Yet her vision beyond remained the same, cloudy and uncertain.

She hadn't heard from Cole since he'd relocated to San Francisco and as much as she needed to hear his voice, perhaps his way was better.

What was it about her that kept her incapable of giving totally, of speaking her real feelings, allowing another's love to help her wounds to heal?

There was so much bottled inside, brimming to the surface, ready to overflow. But each time the words rose to her lips, she'd swallow them back. To allow them to surface, to be spoken, would ultimately reveal her weakness. And weakness, need, had nearly destroyed her once before. And she was terrified to risk that kind of hurt again.

She turned away from the nothingness beyond her line of sight and sat on the chaise lounge.

She understood now what it really was that had happened with her and Ray. It was a coupling, yes. It was the making of love, yes. But more than that, it was the one way she knew to release her inhibitions, shed her armor. And somehow, she believed Ray understood that. Accepted it, even though, she also knew, he wanted more. And if he understood that about her, accepted the flaw of who she was, was he the man for her? The one who wouldn't ask for more than she was willing to give?

It was Cole, in his insistent gentleness, who needed all of her, not just the bits and pieces that remained.

Would she ever be capable of that level of giving, ever again, to Cole or to anyone before it was too late?

In the distance she heard the faint ringing of the doorbell. Raven had gone out earlier, with the intention of spending the dreary Saturday afternoon in the company of her friends.

The relationship between the two of them since Cole's departure had been polite, but distant. In Raven's silence was her loud accusation that it was Leone's fault that Cole was no longer in her life.

Leone missed the warm friendship that she and Raven had begun to build over the past year. Now it was as it had been before, a tenuous truce that with the slightest provocation could be broken.

The bell rang again. Finally she sat up and peeked out of the window. Antoinette's car was parked out front.

Securing the belt of her robe around her waist, she hurried down the stairs to the door. She'd skillfully avoided Antoinette over the past couple of weeks, not yet able to speak the words of confession that she knew her friend would demand to know.

But Antoinette, being who she was, would never allow Leone to sink alone in her own ship of confusion and doubt.

Leone pulled in a breath, pasted on a smile and opened the door.

Antoinette stood there with her head dipped to the side, her hand planted on her full hip.

"I figured the only way we were going to talk was for me to just crash the party in person, since you haven't returned my calls."

"Oh, girl, please. You know how busy I am," Leone said lamely.

"Don't 'oh, girl' me. You gonna let me in or what?"

Leone stepped aside and Antoinette sashayed in, dripping water from her Kenneth Cole umbrella. She deposited it in the silver bucket by the door and stripped out of her raincoat, hanging it on the matching coat rack.

"Where's Raven?" she asked, heading for the living room.

"She went out."

Leone trailed Antoinette inside and took a seat on the couch, tucking her bare feet beneath her.

Antoinette plopped down on the love seat and stared Leone in the face. Suddenly all the fronting was gone. Her face and voice softened. "Tell me what's going on, Lee. That's why I'm here."

Leone's nostrils flared as she took in a reinforcement of air. How could she explain when it was all so twisted in her head?

"Doesn't matter how you put it, just get it out," Antoinette gently coaxed, seeing the lines of tension draw between Leone's troubled eyes.

"He's gone, Nettie." Her voice cracked and her eyes filled. "And I let him. It's my fault. I hurt him and I don't think I can ever make that up to him." She sniffed and heaved in short, staccato breaths.

"What really happened, hon? It's okay. This is me."

Leone pressed her lips together, then leaned her head back against the cushions of the couch, closing her eyes.

Behind her closed lids, all the images of the past few months; from her steady withdrawal from Cole, to Ray's entrance into her life, to the afternoon they came together, to his painfully beautiful musical confession, to the day Cole boarded his plane. The scenes all danced together in an almost macabre frenzy—a movie reel out of control.

One scene faded into the next until they all became one brilliant cacophony of light and sound.

Slowly, Leone told it all, like one in a dream state, leaving nothing out, not her deepest secrets or her worst fears. She confessed her role in it all, succumbed to and accepted the flaw in herself. She shared the pain of loss between her and Raven, Cole, Ray. She told it all until she exorcised all of the demons that had tormented her, leaving her empty, but sadly not cleansed.

When she opened her eyes, Antoinette was seated next to her.

"That's one helluva story, girl," she said, wiping the line of tears off Leone's cheek. "The question is, now that the deeds are done, what are you going to do about it? You can't spend the rest of your life in mourning. You can't let Raven slip away again because you can't get yourself together."

Leone lowered her head.

"The sad reality is, Cole is gone. That was his decision, whether you played a role in that decision or not. You could call him, tell him to come back. But back to what? What's going to be different about you that would make him stay?"

"Nothing at the moment."

"Exactly my point. Like I told you before, Lee, you never really gave yourself time to heal after Steven. Sure time passed, but you never addressed the real issue, you. And until you do that, nothing will ever be any different with Ray, with Cole, with anyone."

"That's comforting," Leone said sarcastically.

"Have you and Ray talked since..."

Leone shook her head. "No. Not really. He's tried. He's asked me out. Wanted to know if he could call me. But I keep putting him off. If I even think for a minute that we might somehow be alone, I find a quick exit."

"That's real womanly, Lee. What are you so afraid of?"

Leone crossed her arms and huffed. "What should I do, then?" she asked, her voice rising in frustration.

"For starters, why don't you see what the man has to say. If he did what you said he did up on stage in front of all those people, he has to be a man of substance. Maybe he'll understand more than you give him credit for. Give him a chance."

Leone was thoughtful for a moment. Ray did deserve to be heard, she reasoned. After all, what happened with them wasn't just about her, and although he seemed to go along with her program, she knew it wasn't how she truly felt. Maybe it was time she really listened.

She blew out a breath. "I'll try."

"That's a start. And at some point, you need to talk with Cole, Lee. Really talk to him, even if it means going out to San Francisco to do it."

She slowly shook her head. "I—I don't know about that, Nettie."

"I'm not saying tomorrow, but at some point. You can't go through life with all the threads trailing behind you. You've got to tie off those loose ends, so they can stop tripping you up."

Leone grinned. "You and your metaphors."

"Hey, whatever works. But one thing at a time."

Leone nodded, then exhaled. "You know, Ray started this jam session thing."

"What's that?"

"We rent out the space on Saturday afternoons before the club opens to let a couple of bands work out. Those that don't have rehearsal space."

"Not bad. Get any takers?"

"Takers! The phone hasn't stopped ringing since the word went out."

"Seems like Mr. Man has a business head on his shoulders, too."

Leone smiled tightly. "Yeah, he does. Last week-end was the first session."

"Did you go?"

"No. But I heard...Ray told me...it went according to plan."

"Oh." Antoinette arched a brow. "You two talk about anything else you haven't told me about?"

"No. I've kept it strictly business."

"Hmm. Nuff said on that subject. But...what about Raven?"

"She's just so angry, Nettie. Angry at me."

"She can't stay that way forever." Antoinette got up and went into the kitchen. "Want something to drink?" she shouted from the other room.

"There's some iced tea in the pitcher. That's fine with me."

Antoinette returned shortly with two glasses and handed one to Leone, who relaxed and took a sip. "At some point you're going to have to find a way to get through to her. You can't sit around and let your relationship with her deteriorate. Whether you realize it or not, your daughter is more like you than you're willing to admit."

Leone frowned. "Raven, like me? No way."

"Raven balls up her feelings inside, never really says what's in her heart. She just acts out. She gets that from you. You are one of the most closed people I know."

"I talk to you."

"Yeah, after I beat you over the head. And Raven talked to Cole. He was her outlet. We all have somebody."

"I never really looked at it like that. I suppose that's why it's always been so hard for us to get along.

We're both too busy hiding our feelings, and never really talk to each other except to lash out and be angry."

"Exactly. She learned all that from you. And you have to be the one to break the pattern."

Leone lowered her head. She was at the root of so much that was wrong. She'd let the circumstances of her life completely reshape her. And ultimately, it had affected her daughter. Casualties of war, she thought morosely.

She turned to Antoinette. "Thank you."

"For what?"

"For knocking me in the head. At some point, I'm going to have to take that first step if I ever want things to get better. But most of all I have to do this for Raven. She's the most precious person in the world to me, Nettie. I don't want to see her grow up to be a bitter woman, incapable of feeling the joys of loving someone and being loved in return."

"The next step is deciding where to begin."

Leone nodded, pondering her options. The phone rang. "Excuse me," she said, getting up to answer the phone in the kitchen.

She returned shortly. "That was Raven. She wanted to spend the night at Terri's house." She shrugged. "I told her we needed to talk."

"And?"

"And...she said, 'Can't we do that when I get home tomorrow? I'm really having a good time here. Terri's mother is showing us how she frames and mats portraits.'"

"So of course you said yes."

"Call me a coward and get it over with. She sounded like she'd rather be with Terri's mother anyway."

Leone crossed the room to the other side and leaned against the mantle.

Antoinette twisted her lips. "Maybe because Terri's mother talks to her, Lee."

Leone glared at her. "And so will I." But even as she defiantly said the words, she wasn't sure how she would ever begin.

TWENTY

For the better part of the night, Leone replayed in her mind the conversation she'd had with Antoinette. The more she thought about how much she could lose by remaining the way that she was—locked inside herself—the more determined she was to take the steps toward change. Raven was her catalyst. Finally, during the early morning hours, too weary to think any further, she drifted off into an exhausted sleep.

By the time she was able to pull her eyes open, the bedside clock showed it to be noon. Slowly she pushed herself up, listening for sounds in the house, and heard none.

Raven had yet to return. But being a teenager, she and Terri had probably stayed up the entire night and were still asleep.

Hmm. When was the last time Raven had invited her friends to spend the night? When had she last spent a full day with her daughter just doing mother/daughter things? She couldn't remember. It had always been easier to just set down rules and have expectations.

Suddenly, she felt terribly sad. She'd become so ladened with her own life, her own sorrows, that she'd completely forgotten that Raven needed her too. Just because she was growing up and didn't need changing or to be fed every two hours didn't mean that she didn't need her anymore. How long had she been in this vacuum that had become her life? Too long.

She swung her legs over the side of the bed and padded barefoot into the bathroom. All that stops as of today, she determined, turning on the shower. Somehow she would find the words to make things right. One by one. Step by step.

Less than a half hour later, she was out the door. She wanted to be in the best frame of mind when she talked with Raven. And being in the club on a quiet Sunday afternoon always helped to clear her head.

She decided to walk. The crisp, early November afternoon was part of the remedy she needed. She inhaled deeply of the sharp air, observed the turning of the leaves that were now a myriad of orange and gold, set against a stark white sky. Changes, she thought. The evolution of time, turning what was into something new, a shedding of the past.

Leone turned up the collar of her trenchcoat against the sudden gust of wind and slid her hands into her pockets. Yes, changes, she thought again.

When she arrived at the club, she was surprised to see the light on inside. She sucked in a breath of annoyance. They'd obviously been left on from the night before, leaving her with an astronomical light bill. Ray was going to hear about this. What if she hadn't come by? They would have stayed on until Monday afternoon when the kitchen staff arrived.

Leone stuck her key in the door and tossed it open. Furious, she stormed inside and found it, as she suspected, empty. Out the window went her thoughts of coming here for some quiet solitude and regrouping. She was too pissed off to think about anything other than snatching the neck of the person responsible. She stomped across the room and stopped short when Ray came from the back, wiping his hands on a towel.

The corner of his mouth curved into that smile of his, a cross between seductive and boyish, depending on the recipient's frame of mind.

"Hi." He came toward her.

Her chin jutted upward. "What are you doing here?" Her heart began to race as he drew closer.

He held up both hands in surrender. "Hey, I'm sorry. I just wanted to go over the schedule for the jam sessions in the upcoming weeks and lay out the numbers for tomorrow's rehearsal." He tossed the towel onto the bar. "I'll be out of your way in a minute, just let me get my things."

She tugged in a breath. "Fine." She spun away and took a seat at a shadowed table in the corner. She could kick herself. There was no reason for her to treat him that way. What had he done besides come there to work and say hello to her when she came in? She tried to swallow down her stupidity but it clung like lint in her throat.

"I'll see you later."

Her head snapped around. She hadn't heard him come up behind her.

"I locked up in the back." He gently worked his jaw from left to right as if he was trying to shake the words loose.

"Thank you," she whispered.

"Not a problem." He slung his bag on his shoulder and moved toward the door.

"Ray." Leone stood. "Wait."

He turned but didn't speak. He looked at her and waited.

"Can...we talk...for a minute?"

"I have something to do."

She swallowed. This was her out. She should just let him go. Forget it.

"It won't take long. I promise." She twisted her hands in front of her.

She watched his expression tense, his eyes narrow in suspicion. He worked his jaw again, contemplating.

He looked briefly at the floor, then moved back in her direction. He stood directly in front of her, forcing her to look up at him.

Ray adjusted his knapsack on his shoulders. "I'm listening."

"Can we sit down?"

Ray pulled out a chair and sat without responding. He dropped his knapsack on the floor between his knees.

Leone searched the room with her eyes, trying to buy some time while she formed the words in her head.

Finally, she focused on her entwined fingers, so symbolic, she realized, of her own life.

"This is really hard for me, Ray." She stole a brief glance at him, catching the unreadable expression on his face. "Umm, that day...at your house, I, uh, I didn't mean what I said."

Ray remained stoically silent. He had no intention of making this easy for her. Not after the emotional hell she'd put him through.

"Aren't you going to ask me about what?" she asked, totally rattled by his uncharacteristically chilly demeanor.

Ray folded his arms, looked at her from beneath his lashes and slowly shook his head.

She blew out a breath. "Fine." She raised her chin in that way Ray found so endearing. "I didn't mean that what happened didn't matter to me," she said in short clips. "I'm not one of those young," she emphasized the word, "non-conventional women you're used to dealing with." Her voice and her eyes softened. "I—I've never done anything...like that before. And, I guess I figured the easiest way not to feel like an inexperienced teenager was to...act like it didn't matter."

Leone swallowed over the tightness in her throat. Finally, she looked him square in the eyes. "It did matter. A great deal."

Ray glanced up at the ceiling for a moment, needing to compose his thoughts and his emotions.

"That's all I ever needed you to say to me, Leone—that it mattered. That I wasn't some quick lay to fill in some empty space."

He pulled his chair closer to the table, the sound of its wooden legs scraping across the floor reverberated throughout the silent space.

"Listen, let me just say this. I care about you a lot, Leone. More than I expected and more than you realized. When I made love with you, it was like some dream of mine had come true. For as long as I can remember, I've wanted to feel the way I did with you when I was with a woman. That what we had was making a difference." He blew out a derisive breath. "When you said what you did, it really blew me away. I guess it was my own past coming back to haunt me."

Leone gave him a tight smile.

"I'm not going to sit here and lie to you, Leone. I want you. I want to be with you, really get to know you, and let you know me." He reached across the table and cupped her chin, gently caressing her jaw line with his thumb. His eyes skimmed over her face. "But I also know that deep inside, your heart is somewhere else, not really with me. I care about you a lot, but I'm not in love with you. Cole is. And you're in love with him."

She looked away and bit down on her lip.

"It's okay, Lee. It is. And I don't want to compete with that. I can't. Cole is a decent man, one of the best I've met in my life. You have no idea how much he sacrificed because of how he feels about you."

Her eyes widened. "What do you mean?"

"That's something you and Cole need to talk about. Whatever went wrong between the two of you that made room for us can still be fixed. It's not too late. I really believe that."

Her eyes filled. "I've made such a mess of things, haven't I?"

He gave her that smile again. "Yeah, you have. But there is a bright side to all this."

"What?" she sniffed.

"I'm still young. I can recover. But you two...well....time is of the essence—"

Leone swatted him on the arm. "What are you trying to say?" She swatted him again.

He held up his hands, begging for mercy. "Nothing, nothing," he laughed between swats. "I swear."

Leone eyed him and pursed her lips. "That's better," she said, fighting down the urge to laugh.

For a few moments they looked at each other with a tenderness reserved for those who have shared intimately of one another, and they knew they'd both be all right.

"We should have done this a long time ago," Ray said soberly.

"I know. And I'm sorry for treating you so badly. You didn't deserve that."

He took her hands between his. "What do you say we just forget the past—well, not everything." He grinned wickedly. "And start from today as friends. Nothing more, nothing less."

A soft smile lit her face. "I like the sound of that."

Ray leaned closer, looking deep into her eyes. "I'll never forget what we shared, Lee. And don't you ever think for a moment that it wasn't important to me," he said, still holding her hands.

"I won't forget either," she whispered.

Gently he touched his lips to hers, once, twice.

The sensation of another presence in the room caused them to suddenly spring apart.

Leone gasped when she saw Raven standing in the doorway staring at them.

"I thought I'd find you here," she said coldly. "I figured I'd stop by so we could talk." Raven's breathing was coming in short bursts. Her throat worked up and down.

Leone slowly rose from her seat as she sensed the explosion that was about to erupt.

"You remember Ray, don't you?"

Ray stood. "Good to—"

"Haven't you taken enough already?" she suddenly lashed out. "First it's Cole's job and now my mother! What did he ever do to you?"

"Raven!" her mother warned, walking toward her daughter.

Raven pointed at Leone. "You just leave me alone. How could you do this? With him? He's young enough to be my big brother. How? That's sick." Leone flinched under the barrage of accusations. "You knew how much Cole loved you and how much he loved me. And you ran him away, just like daddy. I hate you. You always leave me with nothing!"

She whirled away and ran out the door.

For several seconds Leone stood in the shadows of the club, paralyzed with humiliation and by the intensity of Raven's outburst.

"Oh, God," she suddenly expelled, covering her mouth with her hand. "I've got to go get her." She turned back toward the table to get her purse, her vision clouded with tears.

"Slow down, Lee." Ray put his arm around her shoulders and felt her entire body trembling. "I'll go with you."

She turned wide eyes on him. "No. Please." She pressed her hands to his chest. Briskly she kissed his cheek. "Thank you," she said in a hushed voice, turned and hurried out.

TWENTY-ONE

Leone ran out onto the sidewalk and looked frantically from one end of the street to the other. Raven was nowhere to be seen. She turned and headed home.

As Leone walked swiftly along the sidewalk, she wished now that she' driven to the club. She sent up silent prayers that she could find a way to make things up to Raven. Her own insecurities and old scars had not just affected her, they'd affected Raven and Cole. And because of that, she stood the risk of losing the two people most dear to her—for good.

Maybe this whole mess was a blessing in disguise. It had forced her to take a hard look at herself, objectively, and although she didn't like what she saw, she believed she could make the changes necessary for a new beginning.

When she finally reached her street, Leone's heart was hammering as she approached the house.

"Please be there," she whispered as she quickly jogged up the steps. But the instant she put her key in the door and went inside, she knew she was alone.

Dropping her bag on the table in the hall, she went straight to Raven's room in hope that perhaps she'd left a note or something.

She scanned the room in all the obvious places and found what she expected—nothing.

Retracing her steps, she headed for her bedroom, went directly to her nightstand and pulled out her phone book.

She'd made it a point early on to have the phone number of all Raven's friends. She began dialing, starting with Terri.

Twenty minutes later, she hung up the phone for the last time. No one had seen her. Or at least that's what they all said. The only one she hadn't reached was Ron. When the answering machine came on, she opted not to leave a message.

She'd talked briefly with Terri's mother who assured her that if Raven turned up she'd make sure she called.

Leone walked to the window and peered outside. The sun was already settling down behind the buildings. It would be dark soon.

She folded her arms, warding off the sudden chill that had crept up her back. What if Raven had run away? What if she never came back, just to punish her?

Leone pushed her fist to her mouth. Where would Raven go? She didn't have any real money to speak of. Since she'd refused to allow Raven to work after school until she'd gotten the first semester under her belt, she was sustained only by her allowance. Which always had to be replenished before its due date.

She crossed the room, heard a car pull up out front and ran back to the window.

Her hopes quickly dissipated. It was only her neighbor.

There had to be something she could do, she worried, her panic level rising with each passing minute. Right now she didn't even have the luxury of calling

Antoinette, who she was sure by now, was on a train to Washington, D.C. for another computer installation job. As Antoinette's career had grown by leaps and bounds over the last year, she'd turned more and more to Cole.

Had this been any other time of crisis with Raven, she would have called him. He would have calmed her down and worked things out with Raven. She'd grown to depend on him, accepted the fact that he was an integral part of their lives. As much as she reveled in her independence, her sense of freedom, she secretly enjoyed the security of knowing that Cole would take care of things. Take care of her.

The phone rang.

Leone ran across the room before it could ring a second time.

"Hello?" She held her breath.

"Everything okay?"

She plopped down on the bed. "Ray. Hi. No, it's not. She didn't come home."

"Did you—"

"I called everyone," she said, heading off his question. "No one's seen her."

"She have a boyfriend?"

"Sort of. Ron. I called but only got an answering machine."

"She's probably just out walking, Lee. Working things out in her head. She'll be back. She didn't take any of her things, did she?"

An electric charge of fear shot through her. She dropped the phone on the bed and ran down the hall to Raven's room. She pulled open her closet and tried to determine if anything was missing. It all seemed to be in place, the best she could tell.

She checked beneath the canopy bed. Raven's suitcase was still there.

Mildly satisfied, she went back to her room. Seeing the phone on the bed she guiltily remembered that she'd left Ray hanging on.

"Ray, you still there?"

"What happened? I was about to hang up and come over there."

"I'm sorry. When you mentioned missing clothes, I realized I hadn't thought to check her closet and had a panic attack."

"And?"

"It looks like everything is there."

"That's a good sign."

"Is it?"

"Sure. The three times I ran away I took clothes. When I wasn't serious, I just took my basketball."

She held back a chuckle, trying to imagine a young Ray Taylor. "Please don't explain. But I'm sure there's a moral in there somewhere."

"What I'm saying is, wherever Raven decided to go, she doesn't plan to stay." He paused. "She'll be back, Lee. Just relax and be there for her when she comes home. She has some real issues on her mind."

"You really think she'll be back?" she asked, needing to hear the reassuring words again.

"I know so. I'd stack my sax on it!"

"Then it must be true."

"Call if you need me. It's not a problem."

She gulped down her reservations. "Thank you. I will."

"You need to call your mom, Rae," Ron said as they walked hand in hand down South Oxford Street.

"I don't have anything to say to her."

"Maybe it wasn't nothin'. You just blowin' it up."

She snatched her hand away. "You don't get it, do you."

"Get what, Rae? You been blaming your mom for everything that's wrong in your life since I met you."

Raven stopped short and propped her hand on her hip. "She is the cause! My dad left because of her. Cole left because of her. She never really talks to me about anything, just tells me what to do. She never listens."

"Maybe you need to think about somebody besides yourself for a change, Rae. You ain't no kid no more. Your mom is probably feelin' it too."

"Since when are you on her side?"

"It ain't about side, Rae. It's about right." He dug his hands into the pockets of his oversized jeans, pushing them farther down on his narrow hips. "I like you. Like you a lot. You know I'd do anything for you."

Raven loosened her defiant stance and focused on the pavement.

Ron's voice gentled. "Go home, Raven. Talk it out."

She twisted her lips to the side. "How'd you get so smart?"

"Been through it with my old man. Last year of high school. We used to battle about everything."

"Really? You and your father seem so close."

He nodded. "Take my word for it. Being out on the street ain't worth it. Your mom is awright. Give her a shot."

Raven stared at him for a long moment. The prospect of sleeping in Fort Green Park was not an enticing prospect. She knew she couldn't stay with Terri. Her mother would make her call home as soon as she walked in the door.

Raven stretched out her hand. "Walk me home?"

"Not a problem, babe."

Ron took her hand and they walked back toward the house. At the foot of her steps, Ron asked, "You want me to come up with you?"

Raven thought about it for a minute. "No. I should go up by myself."

He nodded. "Cool. I'll call you later then."

"Maybe it's best if you call tomorrow," she said with a crooked smile.

Ron kissed her lightly on the lips. "Just be cool, Rae. And honest."

Raven blew air through her teeth. "I'll try." She turned away and went up the steps.

The instant Leone heard a key in the door, the tight, suffocating feeling she'd lived with for the past few hours finally loosened its hold. She ran to the top of the stairs just as Raven came through the door.

Leone's hand flew to her chest in concert with a gush of air that rushed from her lungs upon seeing that her daughter was safe and in one piece.

Slowly she came down the stairs, meeting Raven at the door.

Raven looked away, not sure what she would see in her mother's eyes. She closed the door behind her. "Hi," she mumbled under her breath.

"Are you okay, Raven?"

Raven tugged on the inside of her mouth with her teeth. "No."

"Neither am I," Leone admitted, and realized that it felt good to say the words.

Raven's smooth brown features bunched into a frown at her mother's admission. In her entire life she couldn't remember her mother ever admitting that anything was wrong, that she ever felt anything other than "fine."

"Come on inside. We need to talk, really talk. Starting with your father." She put her arm around Raven's stiff shoulders and guided her into the kitchen.

In the hours that she'd sat in her room waiting for Raven's return, she'd thought about how to approach the subject of her ex-husband. She could easily sugarcoat it, keep him the invisible hero that Raven believed him to be, or she could simply avoid the entire painful topic as she'd always done.

But she was slowly coming to understand that Raven needed to know the truth. Perhaps not every gory detail, but the truth, so that she could free herself from the fantasy of Steven and see things as they really were. Avoiding the things that hurt, avoiding the issues that raised uncomfortable feelings had been the elements that brought them to this place. Neither of them would ever be whole, be better if it continued. And it was up to her to make the first move.

So, she did. Little by little she spoke of her blind love and faith in Steven, of her own fragile sense of self and how she'd allowed a bad marriage to feed her insecurities.

"I don't believe that your father is a bad person, Raven," Leone said, hoping to put a balm on the wound that she'd opened. "I just think that, unfortunately, the two of us brought out the worst in each other. We fed off each other's weaknesses. And that's not what real love is about."

Leone took Raven's hand. "But my battle didn't stop there. I turned all that hurt and sense of failure as a woman on myself. I withdrew. From you, from my friends, from life." She pushed out a thoughtful breath. "I guess I thought if I didn't ever let anyone get close to me, know my feelings, my thoughts, I couldn't ever be hurt like that again."

"Me, too?" Raven asked incredulously.

"Not intentionally. But questions about your father, questions about how to live, how to be a young woman, make choices; all those things became threats to me."

"Why?"

"Because it reminded me how incompetent I felt about dealing with them."

"So you shut me out, too."

"Yes," she uttered. But her answer was more than a confession, it was a plea for forgiveness. And somehow, Raven in her seventeen-year-old wisdom, understood it.

"And I shut out Cole."

"What are you going to do about that?"

Leone's brows flickered in contemplation. "I'm not really sure yet. I know I need some time to work through some of my issues, try to be more open, willing to share in a partnership before I can think of me and Cole in any concrete way."

"But what if he stays out there and finds someone else?"

"That's a chance I'll have to take. I won't be in another relationship with anyone if I can't be all there. It's not fair to me or to them."

Raven turned a plastic cup around and around on the table. She met her mother's steady gaze. "Ron was right."

"Ron? Right? About what?"

"He was the one who convinced me to come home, to really listen."

"He did?" She couldn't have been more surprised than if she'd won the lottery. She obviously had very much underestimated Ron. Out of the mouths of babes, she thought.

"It's kind of nice, too," Raven paused, "talking like this with you."

Leone felt her heart swell with love when she realized how much she'd missed by shutting out this wonderful young woman from her life. She vowed to never let it happen again.

"I kind of like it, too."

Raven propped her elbows on the table and rested her chin in her palms. "So does this mean we can talk about anything, now?"

Leone's right brow arched suspiciously. "Hmm. I suppose," she said with caution.

Raven waited a beat. "Is there something going on between you and that guy, Ray?"

Leone thought about it for a split second. "No. He's just a friend and a great bandleader. That's it."

Raven angled her head to the side, checking for any chinks in the story. "Okay. Just asking. 'Cause if it was...well, I guess it would be all right. I guess."

"I'm glad I have your blessing, but I don't think it's anything for you to concern yourself with."

They were both silent for a while, caught up in this new relationship they were forging. Finally, Raven spoke.

"I'm sorry about going off like that at the club. That wasn't cool."

"You're right. It wasn't. But you're forgiven. As long as it doesn't happen again." She pinched the tip of Raven's nose, then pushed up from her seat. "I'm starved."

"Me, too. Terri's mom taught us how to make curried chicken," she said excitedly. "Want me to show you?"

Leone's eyes widened in a combination of surprise and alarm. Raven had never set foot in the kitchen for anything more complicated than sitting down to eat, or warming something up in the microwave.

"Sure," she finally stuttered.

Leone watched her daughter move expertly around in the kitchen, taking out all the preparations like a pro. She shook her head and smiled.

Changes. One step at a time.

TWENTY-TWO

For the first time in almost two months since Cole moved to the West Coast, Antoinette had a full day off. She and Leone had been keeping in touch by way of the telephone. So with some down time, they decided that with Christmas only weeks away, they'd spend Saturday morning doing what they considered early shopping.

"I can't remember the last time I actually shopped with more than a week until Christmas," Antoinette commented, examining a silk scarf in Saks Fifth Avenue. She placed her two overloaded shopping bags at her feet.

"You and me both. It's usually a mad dash two days before for me. If I'm lucky. What do you think of this for Raven?" She held up a two-piece pants suit in navy blue.

"Hmm. Raven is so picky about her clothes. I don't know, Lee," she frowned.

Leone hung the suit back on the rack. "You're right. I never know what the latest fad is from one month to the next. Maybe I'd be better off getting her some CDs."

"Now you're really treading on thin ice."

Leone laughed. "True. I can't understand a thing half those so-called singers are singing about."

Antoinette picked up her bags and they continued strolling through the store. "Tell you the truth, I think it's supposed to be that way.

"Yeah. Hey, maybe some boots."

"That's safe." Antoinette peered into a jewelry case lined with gold bracelets. "How are things between you and Raven?"

Leone smiled. "Great, actually. I think the incident at the club was a real turning point—for both of us." She sidestepped a woman with a double stroller. "We talk now. Really talk. And she's not so eager to run out of the house anymore. When I'm home, we actually hang out together."

"That's an improvement." She paused a beat. "What about Cole? Heard from him lately?"

"Not recently."

"Have you tried to contact him?"

"I've thought about it. He sent a card for Thanksgiving and gave me his address and phone number."

"So why haven't you called? You know you miss that man."

They walked toward the exit and out onto the busy Manhattan streets. A light snow had begun to fall, and the mass of humanity moved through it in picture-perfect fashion.

Leone shrugged at Antoinette's question, and tightened the cashmere scarf around her neck. "I don't know. Scared, I guess."

"Of what?" Antoinette jostled her packages and slipped on her gloves.

"That he might not be interested anymore."

"Sorry excuse. You'll never know unless you try."

Leone didn't respond.

"How have things been with you and Ray? Any more sparks flying?"

"Things have been fine with us. And no—no sparks. What happened is in the past. End of story."

"Oh. I was just wondering if maybe that was the real reason you haven't called Cole"

Leone jerked her neck back. "What's that supposed to mean?"

"Let's go into Rockefeller Center and see the tree," Antoinette said, momentarily dodging the question.

But Leone wouldn't let it rest. "Come on, what are you really saying?"

"I'm just wondering if you've really put out the flames with Ray. That maybe you do care about him and think it might interfere—again—if you got back together with Cole."

They walked together in silence as Leone processed Antoinette's comments.

There might have been a time when she would have completely agreed with Antoinette. But not now. She would admit that she did like Ray. They'd developed a solid friendship over the past few months, an honest one. She had no illusions that there was a future for the two of them. Underneath his claim to want stability, Ray Taylor still had some wild oats to sow. He told her as much when they'd shared lunch together several days earlier, which is what she told Antoinette as they entered Rockefeller Center...

She and Ray had gone to her favorite African restaurant on Fulton Street. Leone was determined to get him to try the vegetable pita sandwich, although he swore he was a devout meat eater and marvelous cook, and that vegetables weren't what he considered full course meals.

"This better be good," he grumbled, helping her out of her down coat before taking a seat.

"Just relax and don't be a crybaby." She snapped open her menu for emphasis.

"That's not one of those age jokes, is it?" he quipped, picking up his own menu.

"No, it's an experience joke. You've got to broaden your horizons, try new things," she said loftily.

"Yeah, okay. Just as long as it wasn't an age joke," he replied, wagging a finger at her.

Leone chuckled and shook her head.

Abruptly, he put down the menu and leaned forward, bracing his sweater-covered arm on the table.

"You know what, Lee?"

"Hmm?" she responded absently, still scanning the menu.

"That Sunday...at my house."

Her stomach took a quick dip as her gaze rose above the top of the menu. They hadn't discussed that afternoon since it happened and the resurrection of it suddenly heated her with embarrassment.

"What about it?" *Please don't tell me you have something I could have caught.*

A waitress appeared at the table like an apparition. "What will you both be having?" she asked in a heavy Senegalese accent.

"Uh..."

"She's the expert," Ray said, pointing an accusing finger at Leone. "I'm at her mercy." He flashed Leone a wicked smile and a wink.

"Two steamed vegetable pitas and two salads with carrot dressing." She caught the pained look on Ray's face and added insult to injury by ordering carrot juice.

"Right away," the young woman said, jotting down their orders. She removed the menus and whisked away as quietly as she'd appeared.

"As I was saying..." Ray continued, undeterred.

Now, if she were the old Leone, she would have quickly stated that it was over and done with and she didn't want to discuss it. But if Ray could eat a vegetarian meal, she could live through discussing "that" day.

"Yes."

"I've done a lot of thinking since then, about you, but especially about me."

Leone reached for her glass of water and hoped her hands wouldn't shake. She took a long swallow.

"But you know the one thing we never talked out is why it happened." He reached for his glass as well but didn't drink, only held it in his hand. "You don't have to tell me your reason, but I want you to know mine."

Leone held her breath and waited.

"For a while, even before I met you, I'd begun to feel like my life was running away from me, that I needed to nail it down." He took a breath. "I began to think I was wasting myself, that I needed stability, and having one woman would do the trick. I blamed everything on that..."

The waitress arrived with their salads. Ray curled up his nose, but Leone dug in, needing something immediate to do to keep from hearing some awful truth.

"Anyway," he continued, pushing his salad around with his fork, "when I met you, I locked in on you. I guess because you were so different from any other woman I'd known. Somewhere in the back of my head

I believed being with you would miraculously change me, make things different for me."

She swallowed a forkful of salad, afraid to ask the question that hung on her lips: Did I change your life?

As if reading her mind, he answered. "You did change me. But not the way I'd imagined. What being with you made me realize was that the change has to come from me. I can't hang my hopes on someone else. That's the wrong kind of expectation."

Ray finally took a tiny morsel of salad and moved it around in his mouth. Suddenly his eyes widened in surprise. He dug his fork in again and took a sizeable chunk. "This is actually good," he said, chewing and swallowing.

Leone gave him an arched I-told-you-so expression, but refrained from rubbing it in.

"Anyway," he wiped his mouth with the cloth napkin, "what I'm trying to say is, with you I was able to discover who I was, who I still am. Deep down I love my life the way it is, and when the time is right, the circumstances are right, I'll know it."

"So you're saying I was just an experiment."

"No. Not at all. What I'm saying is, when I'm ready I know what I want."

"What's that?"

"A woman like you, Leone. Don't think any less of yourself because of what happened with us. You're an incredible woman. Any man would be lucky to have you." He reached across the table and put his hand atop hers. "Don't blow it, Lee. Figure out what you want and go after it. You can't get back time lost, but you can still move forward."

Even though he didn't come right out and say it, she knew he was talking about her and Cole.

"That being said," Ray suddenly announced, "I have to break down and admit that this salad is great. If these veggies things taste half as good, I'm hooked."

"Then you're in for a treat. How are the jam sessions going?" she asked, thankful to change the subject.

"Great. Great. As a matter of fact I wanted to run this idea by you."

"Sure..."

"So, you're going to have these blow-out jam sessions during Christmas week," Antoinette enthused. "What a fabulous idea."

"Yep. Ray worked it all out. He has all the groups lined up and we have a reservation list that will take us well past the new millenium!"

"I know you put me down, right?"

"I'll have to check my records," Leone teased.

"Don't play me, girl. Besides, it will give me a chance to meet this Ray character and see what kind of skills he has."

Leone had a brief erotic vision, shook her head and laughed.

The week leading up to the Christmas extravaganza was over-the-top hectic. The entire staff was running around like insane people, barking orders and bumping into each other. The chaos began when word "slipped out" to the press that Soul to Soul would be holding the music event of the year with a week-long array of jazz bands and guest performers, a feat that had never before happened in a local Brooklyn club.

Two television stations had called wanting to tape the shows, and the local cable station, BCAT, would be taping the entire series for continuous broadcast.

The concept had blown up to monumental proportions, and although making all the arrangements and being sure everything was in place was driving her crazy, she loved every minute of it. Raven, Terri and Ron were even pitching in since school was closed for winter recess. Their real reason for being so accommodating was the hope that they'd be seen on television. But Leone didn't mind. She could use all the help she could get, plus it gave her and Raven a chance to bond on yet another level.

Leone had just sat down in her office after spending the morning supervising the painting of the formal dining room, when the phone rang. She exhaled an exhausted breath and picked up the phone.

"Soul to Soul, Leone Weathers speaking..."

By the time she got off the phone ten minutes later, she'd agreed to have the Christmas show broadcast live on WBLS.

She still held the phone in her hand, her thoughts frozen, when there was a knock on the door.

"Come in," she said absently.

Ray opened the door and stepped in, looking GQ perfect in his black ensemble.

"Hi. Listen, I'm going to start the next set of rehearsals in about an hour. Do you think the kitchen would mind doing lunch for them again today?"

"I don't see why not. You want me to ask?"

"If you wouldn't mind."

"Not a problem. Oh, I just got a call from WBLS radio. They want to broadcast the Christmas show live! Can you believe it?"

Ray grinned like a kid. "Of course. This is the event, woman. You're going to be on the map, Lee!" He slapped his hands together.

"Thanks to you."

"Hey, I'm a small piece of the puzzle. Cole was the key to the whole thing. If he hadn't hired me, this would have all been a moot point."

Cole. Her throat tightened. How would she get through Christmas without him? As much as she'd tried to put him out of her mind, she couldn't. There was so much of her life during the time they were together that he had been a part of; from the design of her office to the layout of the club, to the way he smoothed things over with Raven, to the way she drove her car, to how she expected to be treated.

She missed him, dammit. She missed being able to look up and see him walk through the door with that smile of his. She missed his strong fingers instinctively finding all the tension knots in her shoulders. And she missed sitting out in the audience and not seeing him behind the piano, playing something just for her.

"Are you okay?"

Leone blinked, pressing her lips together. "Yes," she said, her voice sounding strained.

Ray looked at her for a long moment and could tell by the wistful look in her eyes what was going through her head.

"Live, huh?"

"That's what they said," she replied, attempting to sound cheery.

"Then I guess we'll have to make it extra special."

Leone looked at him curiously. He winked and walked out.

TWENTY-THREE

Christmas was coming on a Saturday this year. One more day to go and the whirlwind that the past week had been would mercifully be over. Thank the heavens, Leone thought, painfully stepping out of her black heels.

Every night had been a sell-out. Even though they did honor reservations, if guests were more than twenty minutes late, they lost their table. There had been a line down the block and around the corner every single night.

Leone literally collapsed across her bed. She couldn't begin to imagine what tomorrow was going to be like. The local cable station and the radio station people would be there from mid-day on, checking equipment, finding the best locations, and making general nuisances of themselves.

As she drifted off to sleep, still clothed in her Versace cocktail dress, she wondered if fame and fortune was all it was cracked up to be.

After eating a huge Christmas breakfast and ripping open Christmas presents, Leone and Raven dressed in their new cable knit sweaters, jeans and matching boots and headed for the club, their evening wear slung over their shoulders in garment bags.

When they arrived, there was already a line forming in the hope of getting a reservation for the final
performance, which promised to be something to
remember long after the night was over. Ray would-
n't even tell her who the lineup was.

"That's all part of the hype of effective promotion,"
he'd told her when she practically begged for details.
"Give them just enough to whet their appetites." With
that tidbit of information, he'd strolled off with a vic-
torious look in his dark eyes.

Sometimes she could strangle him, she thought as
she and Raven wended their way around the line and
eased inside.

The instant she set foot in the club, it was non-stop
action, from soothing the ruffled feathers of her staff,
the news and radio crews, to checking on menus and
putting in orders for rush supplies of paper goods.

When she sat down to catch her breath, she looked
at the clock and it was already five-thirty. She
dropped her head on her arms and squeezed her eyes
shut. At that precise moment she felt eternally grate-
ful that Cole had had the foresight to install a mini
shower in the office bathroom. It had come in handy
on many a night.

A slow smile spread across her mouth when she
recalled the steamy lovemaking sessions she and Cole
had shared in the office after the staff was gone for the
night. Then they'd squeezed into the narrow shower
stall and start all over again.

She sighed. For the New Year, she was going to
take a trip to San Francisco. The hell with this. She'd
sent him a card for Christmas, but she hadn't heard
from him. Well, she pushed herself up from her seat,
if she had anything to do with it, that was all going to

change. Soon. Come Monday morning, she was going
to the travel agency and purchase her ticket. She did-
n't care if she was going to have to eat crow, she was
going to make all this up to Cole, tell him how much
she loved and missed him and that her life was hell
without him in it.

She took her garment bag from the hook on the
back of the door, locked the door and headed for the
bathroom. A hot shower was just the remedy she
needed at the moment. She had a long night ahead of
her.

∞

From the instant the doors opened for the first set, the
house was packed. Leone had had to hire extra
kitchen staff as well as three more waitresses and two
bartenders in order to handle the crowds during the
past week and it still didn't seem like enough.

She was standing in the back of the room scanning
the glitter of the throng when the house lights dimmed
and Ray took center stage.

"Good evening ladies and gentlemen. As you may
or may not know, I'm Ray Taylor and this," he waved
his hand expansively behind him, "is the Cole Fleming
quintet."

The club erupted into applause. And Leone's heart
thumped in her chest with the mention of Cole's name.

"Thank you." He held up his hand for quiet. "It
was because of Cole and the owner of Soul to Soul,
Leone Weathers," he peered out into the crowd and
upon spotting Leone pointed her out, "that this glori-
ous week of non-stop jazz has been possible. And in

tribute to the both of them I'd like to welcome none other than the incomparable Herbie Hancock!"

Leone's mouth dropped open and the audience went ballistic.

Herbie glided onto the stage, dressed in traditional black with his trademark round, wire-rimmed glasses and took his place behind the piano. He smoothly swung into "Driftin'," which he'd originally recorded with Dexter Gordon on tenor sax. And Ray played his stand-in role with ease.

Heads bobbed and fingers popped. Leone was so excited she thought she'd burst with delight. This was absolutely incredible. Antoinette was out there somewhere with her latest boyfriend, but she couldn't spot her.

The cameras were capturing every minute and the radio station was pumping out every note to the listeners across the city.

Everything was perfect, more than she could have ever imagined. Well, almost perfect. Suddenly she had a wave of melancholia. She looked around the room. Everywhere that her eyes landed she spotted couples, couples. Couples hugging, couples holding hands, couples with their heads close in conversation.

This was the kind of night, the kind of moment you shared with someone important in your life, someone you loved. And for all the glory of the evening, in the total success of the series, she didn't have that one thing that would make it—

"I always wished I could play like Herbie."

Her stomach lurched and her heart seemed to stumble in her chest. The voice was right in her ear, in that familiar spot that would send shock waves running along her body. She was almost afraid to turn around because of what she might not find.

She could feel her legs tremble as she pivoted around, and she looked up into those warm, caring eyes. He wore all gray, the silk sweater stretching across his wide chest. She reached up and caressed his cheek before she spoke, needing the reassurance that he was real and not the lights and sounds playing tricks on her.

"Cole," she whispered.

"Hey, babe." He smiled down at her and even in this crowded room, she was the only one he could see.

"How...when? No one told me."

"Ray found me through the musicians' union."

"Ray?" she asked incredulously.

"Yeah, told me I still had some unfinished business...with you. Is that true, Lee? Is there anything we need to say?" He stroked her shoulder, needing to touch her.

"I love you. I made some mistakes and I want to make it up to you. If you'll let me. I need you, Cole, more than I was willing to admit—because I was scared." She gazed up into his eyes, as Herbie segued into his piano solo version of "My One And Only Love."

Cole ran his finger down her chin. "Do you know how long I've waited for you to say that?"

"Too long. But I promise you, you won't have to wait ever again. I'm going to remind you every day, in every way I can, how much I love you."

Cole slid one arm gently around her waist and pulled her flush against his body. "I'm going to hold you to that," he uttered before lowering his head to touch his lips to hers.

Instantly she felt her spirits soar and she was suffused with an unexplainable joy. She eased closer, reveling in the feel of him. She didn't care who was watching. Because all she could think about at that moment was that she'd been given a second chance.

She'd doubted herself as a woman, a mother, a partner. She'd allowed herself to believe that in order to be whole you needed to be validated by someone else. But it wasn't true. That came from inside. She knew that now. And she thanked her stars above that Cole was wise enough to give her that space she needed to be all she could be—to herself and to him.

Ray stood on the far side of the club, leaning casually against one of the pillars, watching the embracing couple who had all but shut out the world. He smiled with contentment. That's what love was all about, he thought—loving enough to let go.

Raven eased up beside him and gazed happily at her mother and Cole. She looked up at Ray. "Thanks a lot for what you did for my mom and Cole."

Ray slipped his arm around her shoulders. "That's what friends are for. That's what friends are for."

Donna Hill is the reigning queen of African-American romance. Her novel *Indiscretions* (reprinted by Genesis in 1998) was the first ethnic romance to make a national bestseller list.

Donna lives in Brooklyn, New York with her family and works by day as a Public Relations Associate for the Queens Borough Public Library system. She conducts writing workshops and seminars for community colleges and other venues and produces author-centered events under her promotional management company, Annod Productions. She has been featured in *Essence Magazine, Newsday, The Daily News, Publisher's Weekly, Black Enterprise, The Washington Post, The Amsterdam News,* and *USA Today.* She has appeared on BET, "The McCreary Report," "Good Day New York," Lifetime Television, and numerous other cable and radio programs across the country.

INDIGO: Sensuous Love Stories *Order Form*

Mail to:
Genesis Press, Inc.
315 3rd Avenue North
Columbus, MS 39701

Visit our website at

http://www.genesis-press.com

Name _____

Address _____

City/State/Zip _____

1999 INDIGO TITLES

Qty	Title	Author	Price	Total
	Somebody's Someone	Sinclair LeBeau	$8.95	
	Interlude	Donna Hill	$8.95	
	The Price of Love	Beverly Clark	$8.95	
	Unconditional Love	Alicia Wiggins	$8.95	
	Mae's Promise	Melody Walcott	$8.95	
	Whispers in the Night	Dorothy Love	$8.95	
	No Regrets (paperback reprint)	Mildred Riley	$8.95	
	Kiss or Keep	D.Y. Phillips	$8.95	
	Naked Soul (paperback reprint)	Gwynne Forster	$8.95	
	Pride and Joi (paperback Reprint)	Gay G. Gunn	$8.95	
	A Love to Cherish (paperback reprint)	Beverly Clark	$8.95	
	Caught in a Trap	Andree Jackson	$8.95	
	Truly Inseparable (paperback reprint)	Wanda Thomas	$8.95	
	A Lighter Shade of Brown	Vicki Andrews	$8.95	
	Cajun Heat	Charlene Berry	$8.95	

Use this order form
or call:

1-888-INDIGO1

(1-888-463-4461)

TOTAL _____

Shipping & Handling _____
($3.00 first book $1.00 each additional book)

TOTAL Amount Enclosed _____

MS Residents add 7% sales tax

INDIGO *Backlist Titles*

QTY	TITLE	AUTHOR	PRICE	TOTAL
	A Love to Cherish	Beverly Clark	$15.95 HC*	
	Again My Love	Kayla Perrin	$10.95	
	Breeze	Robin Hampton	$10.95	
	Careless Whispers	Rochelle Alers	$8.95	
	Dark Embrace	Crystal Wilson Harris	$8.95	
	Dark Storm Rising	Chinelu Moore	$10.95	
	Entwined Destinies	Elsie B. Washington	$4.99	
	Everlastin' Love	Gay G. Gunn	$10.95	
	Gentle Yearning	Rochelle Alers	$10.95	
	Glory of Love	Sinclair LeBeau	$10.95	
	Indiscretions	Donna Hill	$8.95	
	Love Always	Mildred E. Riley	$10.95	
	Love Unveiled	Gloria Green	$10.95	
	Love's Deception	Charlene A. Berry	$10.95	
	Midnight Peril	Vicki Andrews	$10.95	
	Naked Soul	Gwynne Forster	$15.95 HC*	
	No Regrets	Mildred E. Riley	$15.95 HC*	
	Nowhere to Run	Gay G. Gunn	$10.95	
	Passion	T.T. Henderson	$10.95	
	Pride and Joi	Gay G. Gunn	$15.95 HC*	
	Quiet Storm	Donna Hill	$10.95	
	Reckless Surrender	Rochelle Alers	$6.95	
	Rooms of the Heart	Donna Hill	$8.95	
	Shades of Desire	Monica White	$8.95	
	Truly Inseparable	Mildred Y. Thomas	$15.95 HC*	
	Whispers in the Sand	LaFlorya Gauthier	$10.95	
	Yesterday is Gone	Beverly Clark	$10.95	

* indicates Hard Cover

Total for Books _____

Shipping and Handling_____
($3.00 first book $1.00 each additional book)